Woman.

INTRODUCING
PAGES & PRIVILEGES™.

It's our way of thanking you for buying
our books at your favorite retail store.

GET ALL THIS FREE

WITH JUST ONE PROOF OF PURCHASE:

◆ Hotel Discounts up to 60% at home and abroad

◆ Travel Service - Guaranteed lowest published
  airfares plus 5% cash back on tickets

◆ $25 Travel Voucher

◆ Sensuous Petite Parfumerie collection ($50 value)

◆ Insider Tips Letter with sneak previews of
  upcoming books

◆ Mystery Gift (if you enroll before 6/15/95)

*You'll get a FREE personal card, too.
It's your passport to all these benefits– and to
even more great gifts & benefits to come!*

There's no club to join. No purchase commitment. No obligation.

As a *Privileged Woman,*
you'll be entitled to all
these *Free Benefits.*
And *Free Gifts,* too.

To thank you for buying our books, we've designed an exclusive FREE program called *PAGES & PRIVILEGES™*. You can enroll with just one Proof of Purchase, and get the kind of luxuries that, until now, you could only read about.

*B*IG HOTEL DISCOUNTS

A privileged woman stays in the finest hotels. And so can you—at up to 60% off! Imagine standing in a hotel check-in line and watching as the guest in front of you pays $150 for the same room that's only costing you $60. Your *Pages & Privileges* discounts are good at Sheraton, Marriott, Best Western, Hyatt and thousands of other fine hotels all over the U.S., Canada and Europe.

*F*REE DISCOUNT TRAVEL SERVICE

A privileged woman is always jetting to romantic places. When <u>you</u> fly, just make one phone call for the lowest published airfare at time of booking—<u>or double the difference back</u>! PLUS—

you'll get a $25 voucher to use the first time you book a flight AND <u>5% cash back on every ticket you buy thereafter through the travel service!</u>

FREE GIFTS!

A privileged woman is always getting wonderful gifts.
Luxuriate in rich fragrances that will stir your senses (and his). This gift-boxed assortment of fine perfumes includes three popular scents, each in a beautiful designer bottle. Truly Lace...This luxurious fragrance unveils your sensuous side. L'Effleur...discover the romance of the Victorian era with this soft floral. Muguet des bois...a single note floral of singular beauty. This $50 value is yours—FREE when you enroll in *Pages & Privileges*! And it's just the beginning of the gifts and benefits that will be coming your way!

$50 VALUE

FREE INSIDER TIPS LETTER

A privileged woman is always informed. And you'll be, too, with our free letter full of fascinating information and sneak previews of upcoming books.

MORE GREAT GIFTS & BENEFITS TO COME

A privileged woman always has a lot to look forward to.
And so will you. You get all these wonderful FREE gifts and benefits now with only one purchase...and there are no additional purchases required. However, each additional retail purchase of Harlequin and Silhouette books brings you a step closer to even more great FREE benefits like half-price movie tickets...and even more FREE gifts like these beautiful fragrance gift baskets:

L'Effleur ...This basketful of romance lets you discover L'Effleur from head to toe, heart to home.

Truly Lace ...A basket spun with the sensuous luxuries of Truly Lace, including Dusting Powder in a reusable satin and lace covered box.

ENROLL NOW!
Complete the Enrollment Form on the back of this card and become a Privileged Woman today!

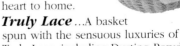

Enroll Today in *PAGES & PRIVILEGES*™, the program that gives you Great Gifts and Benefits with just one purchase!

Enrollment Form

☐ *Yes!* I WANT TO BE A *PRIVILEGED WOMAN.*
Enclosed is one *PAGES & PRIVILEGES*™ Proof of Purchase from any Harlequin or Silhouette book currently for sale in stores (Proofs of Purchase are found on the back pages of books) and the store cash register receipt. Please enroll me in *PAGES & PRIVILEGES*™. Send my Welcome Kit and FREE Gifts -- and activate my FREE benefits -- immediately.

NAME (please print)

_____

ADDRESS   APT. NO

_____

CITY   STATE   ZIP/POSTAL CODE

PROOF OF PURCHASE

SAMPLE ONLY

Please allow 6-8 weeks for delivery. Quantities are limited. We reserve the right to substitute items. Enroll before October 31, 1995 and receive one full year of benefits.

**NO CLUB!
NO COMMITMENT!**
Just one purchase brings you great **Free Gifts** *and* **Benefits!**
(See inside for details.)

Name of store where this book was purchased_____

Date of purchase_____

Type of store:

☐ Bookstore   ☐ Supermarket   ☐ Drugstore

☐ Dept. or discount store (e.g. K-Mart or Walmart)

☐ Other (specify)_____

Which Harlequin or Silhouette series do you usually read?

_____

Complete and mail with one Proof of Purchase and store receipt to:

U.S.: *PAGES & PRIVILEGES*™, P.O. Box 1960, Danbury, CT 06813-1960

Canada: *PAGES & PRIVILEGES*™, 49-6A The Donway West, P.O. 813, North York, ON M3C 2E8

PRINTED IN U.S.A

▶ DETACH HERE AND MAIL TODAY! ▶

Dear Reader,

When I was first invited to write for Temptation's Bachelor Arms miniseries, I thought it might be a good idea if my editor and I visited Los Angeles to research the project. As it turned out, my timing left a bit to be desired. But how could I have known L.A. was due for a major earthquake?

Actually, the trip proved quite an adventure as we went our merry way, taking aftershocks and constant traffic jams in stride. Intrepid researchers, we also browsed the Rodeo Drive stores and ate at the marvelous restaurants frequented by my characters. (The sacrifices we writers make!)

I do hope you enjoy Lily and Mac's romance. Stay tuned for the final episode, *Three Grooms and a Wedding*, where destiny brings Blythe together with the love of a lifetime and the murder of Alexandra Romanov is finally solved.

Happy Reading!

JoAnn Ross

BACHELOR ARMS

Come live and love in L.A. with the tenants of Bachelor Arms

Bachelor Arms is a trendy apartment building with some very colorful tenants. Meet three confirmed bachelors who are determined to stay single, until three very special women turn their lives upside down; college friends who reunite to plan a wedding; a cynical and sexy lawyer; a director who's renowned for his hedonistic life-style and many more…including one very mysterious and legendary tenant. And while everyone tries to ignore the legend, every once in a while something strange happens.…

Each of these fascinating people has a tale of success or failure, love or heartbreak. But their stories don't stay a secret for long in the hallways of Bachelor Arms.

Bachelor Arms is a captivating place, home to an eclectic group of neighbors. All of them have one thing in common, though—the feeling of community that is very much a part of living at Bachelor Arms.

BACHELOR ARMS

THE TENANTS OF BACHELOR ARMS

Ken Amberson: The odd superintendent who knows more than he admits about the legend of Bachelor Arms.

Connor Mackay: The building's temporary handyman isn't telling the truth about who he really is.

Caitlin Carrigan: For this cop, her career is her only priority.

Eddie Cassidy: Local bartender at Flynn's next door. He's looking for his big break as a screenwriter.

Jill Foyle: This sexy, recently divorced interior designer moved to L.A. to begin a new life.

Lily Van Cortlandt: This vulnerable, loving woman can forgive anything other than betrayal.

Natasha Kuryan: This elderly Russian-born femme fatale was a makeup artist to the stars of yesterday.

Gage Remington: Cait Carrigan's former partner is investigating a decades-old murder that involves the residents of Bachelor Arms.

Brenda Muir: Young, enthusiastic would-be actress who supports herself as a waitress.

Bobbie-Sue O'Hara: Brenda's best friend. She works as an actress and waitress but knows that real power lies on the other side of the camera.

Bob Robinson: This barfly seems to live at Flynn's and has an opinion about everyone and everything.

Theodore "Teddy" Smith: The resident Lothario—any new female in the building puts a sparkle in his eye.

JoANN ROSS
FOR RICHER OR POORER

Harlequin Books

TORONTO • NEW YORK • LONDON
AMSTERDAM • PARIS • SYDNEY • HAMBURG
STOCKHOLM • ATHENS • TOKYO • MILAN
MADRID • WARSAW • BUDAPEST • AUCKLAND

If you purchased this book without a cover you should be aware
that this book is stolen property. It was reported as "unsold and
destroyed" to the publisher, and neither the author nor the
publisher has received any payment for this "stripped book."

ISBN 0-373-25641-8

FOR RICHER OR POORER

Copyright © 1995 by JoAnn Ross.

All rights reserved. Except for use in any review, the reproduction or
utilization of this work in whole or in part in any form by any electronic,
mechanical or other means, now known or hereafter invented, including
xerography, photocopying and recording, or in any information storage
or retrieval system, is forbidden without the written permission of the
publisher, Harlequin Enterprises Limited, 225 Duncan Mill Road,
Don Mills, Ontario, Canada M3B 3K9.

All characters in this book have no existence outside the imagination of
the author and have no relation whatsoever to anyone bearing the same
name or names. They are not even distantly inspired by any individual
known or unknown to the author, and all incidents are pure invention.

This edition published by arrangement with Harlequin Enterprises B.V.

® and TM are trademarks of the publisher. Trademarks indicated with
® are registered in the United States Patent and Trademark Office, the
Canadian Trade Marks Office and in other countries.

Printed in U.S.A.

Prologue

Hollywood 1933

THE INSTANT SHE SAW HIM, across the crowded room, Alexandra Romanov knew she'd found her soulmate.

Their eyes—hers a gypsy dark jet, his a riveting sky blue—met, then locked. Everything and everyone in the gilded ballroom of the famed Biltmore Hotel seemed to blur, save for one man, looking so handsome, so splendorous, in white tie.

She caught her breath at his blatant masculinity. The congenial party conversation surrounding her became a distant buzz in her ears. Feeling as if her feet had been nailed to the dance floor, Alexandra could only stand there, like some primitive sacrificial virgin awaiting ravishment by a virile all-powerful god.

She knew who he was, of course. Everyone in Hollywood had been talking about Patrick Reardon, the tough-talking, hard-drinking, poker-playing writer Walter Stern had brought to Hollywood to pen the screenplay of his latest bestselling novel for Xanadu Studios.

Without taking his eyes from her face, Patrick began walking toward her. The crowd between them parted before him like the waters of the Red Sea. Obviously she was not the only person present capable of recognizing such masculine superiority.

He stopped so close to her that the toes of her gold brocade high heels were touching the pointed toes of his boots. The fact that he'd dare to wear cowboy boots with a dinner jacket told Alexandra that this was not a man who bowed to any of society's restrictive conventions.

He took her hand, engulfing it in one a great deal larger and darker. She could feel the row of calluses on his palm.

"I'd tell you that you're the most beautiful woman here tonight," he said, on a low, husky voice. "But you undoubtedly know that."

Alexandra couldn't answer. Her mouth had gone as dry as the desert set where she'd just finished her latest film, a melodramatic epic about a woman taken captive by a sexy sultan.

"I could also tell you that I want you." He ran a finger up the inside of her arm, leaving an enervating, yet exciting trail of sparks on her bare skin. "But you undoubtedly know that, as well."

This time, she managed a nod.

Either oblivious or uncaring of the others, who were watching with undisguised fascination, he brushed the back of his free hand up the chiseled line of her cheekbone. It was all she could do not to turn her head and press her lips against that tantalizing, wicked hand.

"So," he said, "what are we going to do about this?"

The unmistakable desire in that rumbling voice made her knees weak. The scent emanating from his dark skin was not any expensive male cologne, but pine soap that reminded her of the forests back home in her native Russia.

Alexandra knew that if she was to leave with Patrick she would infuriate her escort, Walter Stern, owner of Xanadu Studios. A possessive man, Walter treated her like the rest of his expensive playthings.

Despite her continuing refusal to sleep with him, in all other ways, Alexandra had allowed Stern to become her absolute lord. He supervised her scripts, approved every morsel of food that passed between her ruby lips; he chose her clothing, her hairstyles, her cars, her house and her friends.

A cruel man with the inborn instincts of a tyrant, Walter Stern patronized her, taunted her and sometimes humiliated her. But he'd also taken a nobody and, with the mysterious, infinite gifts of a creator, had breathed life into her nothingness, fulfilling his promise to make her a star.

Unreasonably tempted by this dark and dangerous cowboy who had so intrigued this single-industry town since his arrival, Alexandra understood the dangers of such impulsive behavior.

But generations of passionate, hot-blooded cossacks and earthy, tempestuous peasant women ran deeply in her veins. She knew, with every fiber of her being, that she could not have resisted this man if she'd wanted to.

Which she didn't.

She smiled up at him. A slow, sensual smile familiar to Alexandra Romanov's legion of fans all over the world. A smile that turned her eyes to gleaming ebony, made a man think of voluptuous gypsies dancing around smoky campfires, and promised infinite erotic delights.

"I'd say," she said, her Russian accent thickened by rising passion, "that it's a lovely night for a moonlight drive."

They left the ballroom hand in hand, followed by an excited buzz. Just outside the double doors, gossip mavens Hedda Hopper and Louella Parsons practically came to blows at the single pay telephone.

Patrick led her to the Rolls-Royce convertible the studio had given him when he'd first arrived in Hollywood. The white car gleamed like alabaster in the slating silver moonlight. He dismissed the uniformed chauffeur, taking the keys himself.

As he helped her into the wide leather seat, Alexandra knew that there would be a price to pay for her impetuous behavior. But, like the memorable character Vivien Leigh had recently portrayed for MGM, Alexandra decided she would think about that later. Tomorrow.

Fortunately, as they drove out of the parking lot, headed down Sunset Boulevard toward the moon-spangled Pacific Ocean—and their brief, tempestuous, ultimately fatal future together—tomorrow looked very far away.

1

THE DAY BEFORE the wedding—the wedding of Blythe Fielding to Dr. Alan Sturgess—dawned as bright and sunny as a Los Angeles travel poster. The sky overhead was a clear robin's egg blue, with not a cloud in sight; birds were chirping as they played musical branches amidst the orange trees surrounding the house and a soft sea breeze drifting in from the nearby Pacific carried a faint aroma of salt water.

Later, looking back on what happened, Lily Van Cortlandt would realize that there had not been even the faintest hint of the disaster waiting to strike.

She'd come to California to take part in her best friend Blythe Fielding's wedding. Plagued by nightmares, she'd risen early on that day, showered in the bathroom adjoining the guest bedroom of Blythe's Beverly Hills home, then dressed in a pair of white shorts and a red-and-white striped maternity top.

Perhaps it was due to her lack of sleep, or all the stress she'd been under lately, but for whatever reason, Lily was feeling decidedly edgy.

Thinking a sunrise might be calming, she tried sitting on the balcony outside the French doors of the bedroom. But nerves had her unable to sit still for very long.

Deciding that what she needed was a change of scenery, she crept downstairs, being careful to avoid waking anyone, and called a taxi. After leaving Blythe a note so she wouldn't worry, Lily met the cab out by the driveway gate and had it drop her off at the Malibu pier, where she spent the next hour sitting on a rock, watching the breakers roll in.

Their unceasing, undulating ebb and flow proved wonderfully soothing. The glassy, sun-brightened waters of the Pacific were so vast that somehow they made her own problems seem somewhat smaller by comparison.

Having grown up in Iowa, with a stop in Rhode Island for four years at Brown University before moving to Connecticut as a bride, Lily had almost forgotten how she'd fallen in love with the sea during her visits to Blythe's home during their college days.

Lily loved the sight of the ocean—the vast blue expanse of water topped by white ruffles, the way it sparkled diamond bright beneath a benevolent sun, or turned dark and deep and dangerous whenever a storm would blow in from beyond the horizon.

She loved the smell of it—of fish and salt and myriad, mysterious scents drifting in from faraway exotic lands. She loved the sound of it—sometimes a low, wonderfully rumbling roar, other times, a soft whisper that reminded her of two lovers sharing secrets in the dark.

She loved everything about the Pacific ocean. But most of all, she loved its paradoxes. The magical way it could be both soothing and exciting at the same time.

Drawn to the frothy wide surf, she kicked off her sneakers and waded out into the water. For the first time in weeks, Lily began, ever so slightly, to relax.

She could almost—but never quite—forget the terror she'd felt when served those hateful papers from her in-laws. Although she'd had difficulty wading through the long paragraphs of legalese, Lily had gotten their meaning, loud and clear. Now that their only son had died,

James and Madeline Van Cortlandt intended to fill the hole in their family with Lily's unborn child.

The wet sand, hard packed at the water's edge, oozed between her toes as she waded out farther into the surf. Sea foam swirled around her ankles. The early morning breeze fanned her hair, cooled the back of her neck and left her feeling marvelously liberated.

The ebbing tide left a swath of silvery, shell-strewn sand. Entranced, Lily followed the sea as it slipped back toward the horizon. Immersed in her solitary morning pleasure, she was unaware of the man standing on the edge of the cliff, a man who had been drawn by the sight of the young woman wading through the white sea foam.

She reminded Connor Mackay of a sea sprite. From her retreating figure he could see that although she was not tall, her legs looked long and lean in a pair of crisp white shorts. Her long blond hair, touched by the glow of early morning sunshine, streamed out behind her, like a platinum flag.

Even if he hadn't had his own personal reason to be celebrating this morning, the sight of her would have made him smile. Almost believing in mermaids for the first time in his life, Connor headed down the stone steps to the beach.

Admiration gradually turned to mild concern, then alarm as he noticed she'd wandered into an area marked by riptide warning signs. She was also too far out. The water was now swirling to her knees. And higher.

"Is she blind?" he asked the empty beach. Surely she'd seen the bright orange warning signs. "Or just an idiot? Doesn't she realize the danger?"

As she continued to wade farther out, in the direction of a rock jetty, another, horrifying thought occurred to Connor. Perhaps she knew the perils of this particular stretch of beach. Perhaps her flirtation with danger was not carelessness.

"Aw hell," he ground out, as he looked past her at the enormous breakers swelling on the horizon. If the lady *was* suicidal, she'd picked a damn good spot to end it all.

He began running toward the water.

Humming along with the music playing in her head, Lily paused as a departing wave left a treasure trove of sparkling white shells in front of her. Engrossed in admiring nature's artwork, she failed to see the huge dark wall of water growling its way toward her.

Without warning, it knocked her to her feet, burying her beneath what felt like tons of churning water and gritty sand.

Disoriented, she began to be tossed about like a frail shell, thrown head over heels over head again in a series of somersaults that left her not knowing which way was up. Or down. She only knew that there was a roaring in her ears and her lungs felt as if they were going to burst.

She struggled to stand up, but as she did so, a riptide, coming off the jetty, began pulling her with a deadly force out to sea.

Goddammit! Connor cursed viciously as he watched her disappear beneath the foaming, roiling water. One of two things were going to happen to her. The idiot was either going to be pulled out to sea and drowned, or she was going to be thrown against the stone jetty, breaking every bone in her body.

Diving headfirst into the surf, he began swimming toward the spot he'd seen her last.

Lily absolutely refused to drown. She'd survived too much these past months to give up now.

She thrashed her arms and legs in a modified crawl stroke, fighting against the deadly riptide. Just when she was certain her lungs were going to burst, she felt a pair of strong arms wrap around her with the strength of tentacles. The next thing she knew she was being dragged through the churning surf, back toward the safety of the beach.

Swearing creatively, Connor half carried, half dragged her up onto the packed sand.

"Dammit, what the hell did you think you were doing?" he roared, loud enough to be heard over the surf.

Feeling as if she'd swallowed half the sea, Lily was coughing too hard to answer.

He curled his hands around her upper arms and dragged her to her feet. "You are not only an idiot, lady," he ground out between his teeth on a whiplash voice that made her wince. "You're dangerous. Do you realize your stupid stunt could have gotten us both killed?"

Although he had come to her rescue, the man certainly wasn't Lily's idea of a white knight. Having made the decision never to allow any man—even one who'd just saved her life—to mistreat her ever again, she shook off his touch, stood up straight and met his blistering glare straight on.

"I don't recall asking you to dive into that surf," she reminded him with a toss of her head. "And although I may be a little vague about current California etiquette, I don't believe that playing lifeguard entitles you to yell at me."

Adrenaline was pumping fiercely through his veins, Connor gave her credit for holding her ground. The way she stuck her chin out demonstrated a strong will and as difficult as it was to maintain a sense of dignity while dripping wet, somehow, the lady was managing to pull it off.

He swept his gaze over her and belatedly realized that she was not nearly as lissome as she'd appeared from behind. Her wet cotton top clung to her bulging stomach, revealing her to be very, very pregnant.

"Damn." He shut his eyes. Terrific move, Mackay, cussing out a suicidally depressed, expectant mother. "I'm sorry."

He looked so shocked, Lily almost smiled. Even as she admitted that it was very small of her to enjoy his obvious discomfort, she thought he looked rather appealing when he was embarrassed.

"That's all right," she offered magnanimously. "After all, you did save my life."

Connor wondered if she was angry with him about that, then wondered why he was worried she might be. "Still, I had no business shouting at you."

Lily had never been the type of woman who enjoyed making a man crawl. She was on the verge of assuring her rescuer that she certainly wasn't going to blame him for a very human response—after all, he could have drowned in that deadly riptide as well—when delayed shock set in and she began to tremble.

When she pressed her palm against her belly, Connor, who paid attention to such things, noted she wasn't wearing a wedding band. "Would you mind . . ." Before she could finish asking him if they could continue this conversation sitting down, Lily's rubbery legs began to slowly fold. Only Connor's quick reflexes kept her from falling down.

He scooped her up. Then, holding her against his chest, carried her back across the beach to the cliff, placing her gently onto the sand. "Better?"

"I think so." She lowered her forehead to her bent knees and closed her eyes.

"You know," he suggested on a gentle tone that was worlds different from his earlier furious one, "no matter how dark things look, suicide is never the answer." Having scant idea how to soothe, Connor reached out and awkwardly ran his hand down her wet, tangled hair.

It took a moment for his words to sink in. Realizing he actually believed she had been trying to kill herself by walking into the sea, like some tragic Victorian heroine abandoned by a faithless lover, and belatedly understanding why he'd been so furious at her, Lily opened her eyes.

"I certainly wasn't..." As her gaze locked with a pair of eyes so dark as to be almost black, Lily turned suddenly mute.

Even as she knew she was staring, she couldn't quite help herself. Lord, he was handsome! His wet hair was lush and dark. His jaw was nicely square, but not as surgically chiseled as those ridiculously sexy male models gracing the pages of the beefcake calendars that seemed all the rage these days. He was wearing a black polo shirt and jeans. His clothes, like hers, were soaked.

"I wasn't trying to kill myself. It was an accident."

He stared at her for a long, silent moment, giving Lily the impression that he was trying to read the truth in her eyes.

"I'm glad to hear that," Connor said finally. As his eyes met her wide blue ones, Connor was suddenly struck with an image of the two of them, lying on the beach, bodies pressed close together, like Burt Lancaster and Deborah Kerr in the movie he'd seen just last night on cable in his hotel room.

"Do you live around here?"

Was it her imagination? Or did he actually sound hopeful?

Shaking off the strange sexual fantasy that had just flashed through her mind—a fantasy that involved the two of them rolling around in the surf in a way that was far more dangerous than mere drowning—Lily reminded herself that at seven months pregnant, she was not very appealing.

Dream on, she laughed at herself. Her midwestern roots had resulted in her always having been an extremely down-to-earth type of person. Replaying a scene from an old movie was for other, more glamorous women. Women like Blythe.

"I'm from Connecticut," she said, relieved when her voice didn't reveal the quick hitch in her heartbeat. "I'm here for a friend's wedding."

"Is your husband in town with you?" In L.A., the lack of a wedding ring on a pregnant woman wouldn't be that unusual. But Connor figured people were undoubtedly more conservative in Connecticut. "We should probably call—"

"My husband's dead."

"I'm sorry." As soon as he said the words, Connor knew he was lying. The ugly truth was he was strangely glad the lady didn't have a husband waiting for her.

You're a rotten son of a bitch, Mackay, he told himself.

Not wanting to get into a discussion about the details of Junior's untimely demise, Lily merely shrugged.

"Then we'd better call your friend to come get you," Connor suggested.

"Oh, no! She has so much to do today. I can call a cab."

Connor thought of the jet waiting for him at the executive terminal at LAX. Remembered responsibilities waiting for him back in San Francisco. But he was not willing to let this pregnant mermaid get away. Not yet.

"You've had a shock," he insisted. "And in your condition—"

"My condition?" Lily tossed her head and rolled her eyes toward the vast blue sky. She'd received much the same treatment from Blythe ever since her friend first met her at the airport. "Why is it everyone insists on behaving as if pregnancy is not a perfectly normal female situation?"

When he'd pulled her from the surf, she'd looked fragile enough to shatter. Now, a flash of irritation made her eyes flash like sapphires and brought some much needed color to her cheeks. Unreasonably tempted to brush his fingertips against that rosy flush, he merely lifted a brow.

"I wouldn't know about everyone else, but speaking for myself, I can honestly say that most pregnant females of my acquaintance don't suddenly decide to take up body surfing."

He had a point. But she was not quite prepared to concede it out loud. "Know a lot of pregnant females, do you?"

"Actually, now that you bring it up, mermaid, you're my first."

His low deep voice did funny things to her nervous system. There was a fluttering in her stomach she was afraid had nothing to do with the baby. Lily wondered if he was married. Then reminded herself it was none of her business.

The frank, assessing way he was looking at her reminded Lily of the way a man might study a new, bright red sports car he was considering buying. He had the look of a man who was vastly comfortable with the opposite sex. A man who'd been born knowing the right moves, the right words to coax a woman into his bed. Not that it probably took much coaxing.

Even if she was interested—which she definitely wasn't—Lily realized that this man was way, way out of her league.

"Well, then." Her breath, not at all steady, was coming a little too fast for comfort. "I'd say you're not exactly an expert on the subject of pregnant women."

"True enough. But, since we've already agreed that I saved your life, I can't help feeling responsible for you."

"That is truly ridiculous."

Connor shrugged. "So sue me. It's the way I feel."

Ever since her parents' deaths last year—coming home from a Saturday night dance at the Grange, their car had been struck by a tractor-trailer rig after the driver had fallen asleep at the wheel—Lily was quite literally all alone. Except, she reminded herself firmly, for her baby.

Connor watched as her morning glory blue eyes turned absolutely fierce and realized that they were suddenly wading in deep conversational waters. There was a hell-luva lot more to this pretty blond widow than met the eye. The color deepened in her cheeks, like the prize-winning azaleas that his mother had cultivated in the garden of her Pacific Heights mansion.

Forgetting he wasn't a man who touched people—especially people he didn't know—Connor plucked a piece of seaweed from her hair. It was a casual, unthreatening touch, but as his hand brushed against her shoulder, both Lily and Connor felt the jolt of contact.

"If you won't let me call someone, I'm going to insist on driving you back to your friend's house myself."

The thought was shockingly tempting. Worried that if she stayed here another moment, she'd find herself agreeing to anything this man suggested, Lily struggled to her feet.

"That's not necessary."

He'd touched a nerve, Connor realized. Which made them even. He rose with a fluid, easy grace that made Lily all too aware of her own ungainly body.

"Now there's where you're wrong." His smile was warm and friendly and fatally sexy. "My mother would never forgive me if I abandoned a mermaid in distress."

Without asking permission, he laced their fingers together and began walking toward the cliff stairs.

"*My* mother taught me never to get into a car with strangers," Lily returned.

He laughed at that. A rich, mellow sound that shimmered its way beneath her skin and tingled at her nerve endings. "Sounds as if we just hit a stalemate. How about we compromise and call a cab?"

"And just leave your car in the parking lot?"

"Don't worry, I can come back and pick it up after dropping you off."

The words were laced with an easy self-confidence that had Lily believing him. "Do you always get what you want?"

"Most of the time." His dark eyes were amused.

Having had her fill of selfish, spoiled males, Lily tugged her hand free. "That must be nice."

They'd gone beyond the deep water and were now swimming around in conversational riptides, Connor realized. "It beats the alternative."

She made a muffled sound that could have been reluctant agreement. Or a curse.

Undeterred Connor plunged bravely on. "Tell me, do you mermaids have names?"

"Of course." Even over the sound of the surf, he heard her slight sigh. "It's Lily. Lily Van Cortlandt."

The name rang an instant bell, telling Connor everything he needed to know. He'd gone to school with her husband. He vaguely remembered the grapevine saying something about Junior having married some wide-eyed, green as new grass farmer's daughter. He also recalled that the man he'd known as an egocentric playboy had recently died in a car wreck.

He'd not been alone. A woman had been with him—his administrative assistant, who'd remained in a coma for weeks before finally succumbing to her injuries.

"Lily," he said, thoughtfully. "I like it."

It also suited her, Connor decided as they walked to the top of the cliff. It was simple and pretty and old-fashioned.

"I think this is where you tell me your name," Lily prompted.

It was Connor's turn to sigh. After a rocky start, they'd begun getting along pretty well. And although he was not exactly that reclusive multimillionaire the press was always portraying him to be, he feared her husband may have mentioned their last regretfully unpleasant business dealing. He'd been against including his former schoolmate in the limited real estate partnership, but the others—his attorney, a circuit court judge and a developer of computer software—had insisted that Junior's New York money ties would prove beneficial.

Unfortunately, the deal had fallen apart, but not before Junior proved himself to have very sticky fingers. Connor figured Lily wouldn't exactly be thrilled to learn that she was holding hands with the man who'd filed a lawsuit against Junior Van Cortlandt's estate.

Acting on impulse, as he so often did, Connor decided not to risk ruining the mood. "My friends call me Mac," he lied deftly. "Mac Sullivan." He figured, rightly so, that his maternal grandmother would hit the roof if she'd known he was borrowing her surname—which happened to also be his middle name—to lie to a young, pregnant woman.

It was a nice name, Lily thought. A strong, masculine name without any numbers after it. She frowned, remembering her mother-in-law informing her that the firstborn sons in each generation of Van Cortlandts were always named James Carter. Her husband, although familiarly known as Junior, had been a third. She had no intention of adding a fourth to the list.

He called for the taxi from a pay phone. Although instinct told Lily that she had nothing to fear from this man, common sense told her that to get into a car with any stranger, no matter how handsome or charming, could prove fatal.

The taxi arrived in minutes, driven by a hunk with sunbleached hair. When he flashed a smile at her, Lily thought he looked vaguely familiar.

"Nice neighborhood," Connor murmured when Lily gave Blythe's Beverly Hills address to the driver after they'd settled into the back seat of the cab.

"The house belongs to Blythe Fielding," Lily revealed. "We were roommates in college. At Brown."

To movie audiences all over the world, Blythe Fielding was, at age 25, already a legend. Having won her first acting role as an Ivory soap baby while still in her cradle, she'd been cast in her first role on a television soap opera before her first birthday.

After her character's tragic demise by sudden infant death syndrome, Blythe's agent quickly moved her into feature films. By the time she'd reached adolescence, her fee per picture had hit the six-figure mark.

She'd taken four years off to go east to college, which was where Lily had first met her, along with Blythe's best friend from childhood, Cait Carrigan.

After graduation, Lily had gotten married and moved to a sprawling house with a rolling front lawn and the requisite three-car garage in Connecticut, while Cait and Blythe returned to Los Angeles.

Turning her back on the movie business she'd grown up in, Cait had joined the police force while Blythe discovered that her audience hadn't forgotten her during her absence.

Her adult career had taken off like a comet and was still soaring.

To her international legion of fans, Blythe Fielding was a superstar. To Lily, she was a dear and valued friend.

When the memory of those halcyon college days made her smile, Connor realized that Junior Van Cortlandt had proven stupid to the end. Only an idiot would continue to play around when he had this woman waiting for him at home.

"Blythe Fielding's getting married?" He arched a brow, wondering why, as the new owner of Xanadu Studios, he hadn't been informed of the pending marriage of one of the studio's biggest stars.

"I shouldn't have told you that," Lily murmured. "She's trying to keep it a secret."

"My lips are sealed." Even as he made a mental note to send a gift, Connor mulled the idea over, trying to decide what effect the marriage of America's premiere sex symbol might have on box office sales. "Although this will undoubtedly break hearts all over America."

Although Lily was accustomed to men being attracted to Blythe's sultry looks, she felt a quick stab of something that felt uncomfortably like jealousy.

"Yours included?"

"Actually, I've always been more attracted to women with eyes the color of a sunlit sea and hair the hue of winter wheat."

His warm gaze moved slowly over her face, drifting down to those full, sexy lips, where they lingered, as if he were imagining the taste. Lily's mouth went dry.

"How about hair with half the sea tangled in it?" she asked cheerfully in an attempt to keep things light.

Connor flashed her a devastating grin as he tugged on the damp ends. "My favorite kind."

Confused and wary, Lily lowered her lashes. It had been a very long time since she'd felt a man's touch. An eternity since any man had made her feel desirable.

Neither spoke on the short drive to Beverly Hills. When the taxi reached the driveway, Lily leaned out the back window and punched in the code that caused the gate to obediently open.

Although she hadn't expected such service, no sooner had they pulled up in front of the house than the driver was out of the cab to open the back door.

She opened her mouth to thank him, but before she could say a word, he'd shoved a glossy eight-by-ten in her direction. His name and Screen Actors' Guild number were printed on the bottom of the photo.

"My name is Brent Langley," he said with another flash of teeth that suddenly reminded Lily of where she'd seen him. He'd briefly played the role of a college jock on "All Our Tomorrows," a daytime soap she watched from time to time. "If you could just give my picture to Ms. Fielding and tell her that I'd love a chance to audition for the part of Patrick Reardon in her upcoming project, I'd really appreciate it."

"Shouldn't your agent be contacting her?" Lily asked.

"Oh, he already has. But she hasn't called back, so I thought I'd take this opportunity to have a friend put in a good word for me."

"I'll give her the photo," Lily agreed. "But I can't promise anything."

In truth, she couldn't imagine a more unlikely casting. Patrick Reardon had been darkly handsome and had radiated a dangerous, edgy kind of passion that even the most careful woman would be unable to resist. This sun-bleached, buffed up kid with the toothpaste commercial smile was much more suited to a remake of one of those teenage beach party movies.

"That's all I can ask," he said, bestowing another one of those cute, utterly harmless, boyish grins on her.

Connor, who'd found the exchange vaguely amusing, cleared his throat, ending the sales pitch. He walked Lily to the oversize, carved front doors.

"Well." Lily looked up at him. For some reason she found herself in no hurry to leave.

"Yet another deep subject," he said in a way that had her smiling.

"Yes." The silence lingered. Tension was beginning to build. "Well, thanks again." She held out her hand. "I really do owe you for rescuing me from that riptide."

He enclosed her hand in both of his and wondered if the rest of her skin would be so soft and smooth. "It was my pleasure."

Although he'd never done it before in his life, Connor lifted that silky hand to his lips. "How long are you going to be in town?"

The light touch of his lips against her fingertips was like a silken brand, sending heat shimmering all the way to her toes. When her baby turned a sudden somersault, Lily wryly decided she had to be carrying a girl. She doubted if there was a female of any age capable of resisting Mac Sullivan's magnetism.

"I'm not quite certain." Their eyes met over their joined hands. Lily thought that looking into those deep jet eyes was strangely like being hypnotized.

Seizing the moment, Connor said, "Look, I'm in L.A. from the Bay area on business. But I'll be back next month." As he found himself being seduced by those wide, soft-focused eyes, he contemplated sending the plane back to San Francisco without him. "Did your mother have any rules about having dinner with strange men?"

He was seducing her. With only those deeply set eyes and the soft touch of his thumb, stroking small circles on the sensitive skin of her palm. As a liquefying pleasure seeped into her bones, Lily felt unreasonably tempted.

Annoyed at herself for succumbing to a smooth line and a tender touch, Lily pulled away. "I'm sorry. I don't know how long I'll be staying."

"Next week then." Although he'd never had need to beg a woman, Connor was desperate enough to do so now.

"I don't think—"

"Tonight." The hell with the plane and his plans. One of the secrets of Connor Mackay's enormous success was his ability to punt when a game plan began to fall apart.

"I'm sorry. But I don't date."

"I can understand if you feel it's too soon to get involved after your husband's death, but I was only suggesting dinner. Or a movie, or—"

"No." Her face closed up. "You don't understand. I don't go out socially."

He lifted a brow. "Not at all?"

It was better, Lily told herself, to set the ground rules right off the bat. "Not at all. Not now." She turned around and rang the doorbell to summon the housekeeper. Inside the house a medley of chimes sounded. "Not later. Not ever."

Connor was definitely not accustomed to being turned down. Especially by a woman who, let's face it, he told himself, although she might be lovely, in an old-fashioned, renaissance Madonna sort of way, probably didn't receive a whole lot of offers.

"But—"

"I really am sorry." Her soft smile was sincere, echoing her words. "I'm sure you're a very nice man. And you did save my life. But I'm really not going to change my mind."

The front door opened. "Besides, it's obvious that you're rich. And I have a hard-and-fast rule about getting involved with rich men."

Connor could only stare at her as she turned away and disappeared into the house. It was the first time in his thirty-one years that any woman had claimed to object to his money and even sensing that her ridiculous rule had everything to do with that dead jerk she'd been married to, he still couldn't quite believe she meant it.

The carved oak door closed, effectively shutting Connor out.

It was just as well, he told himself as the actor-cum-cab driver returned him to where he'd left his rental car.

He had enough on his plate right now. He certainly didn't need to get mixed up with Junior Van Cortlandt's very pregnant widow.

Even if the lady did have world-class legs.

2

AFTER ASSURING BLYTHE that she all was right, albeit a bit sandy, Lily went upstairs, took another shower and tried to tell herself that she wasn't regretting, even a little bit, sending Mac Sullivan on his way.

And even as she knew that was a lie, Lily reminded herself that the next two months were going to be difficult enough without allowing herself to get distracted. And Mac Sullivan, she feared, could be a very powerful distraction.

She found Blythe in the sunroom, sitting at a white wicker table, staring outside the floor-to-ceiling windows at the rose garden, which was in full bloom. She appeared far away, lost in contemplation and from the frown on her face, Lily hoped she was not thinking about her upcoming wedding.

"Feeling better?" Blythe's smile—which had been known to make men in theaters all over America hot—was warm and sincere. Her dark eyes were laced with friendly concern as they moved over Lily's face.

"I wasn't feeling that bad," Lily lied. "Just wet." Having viewed the shadows beneath her eyes in the bathroom mirror this morning and sensing Blythe was about to challenge the obvious prevarication, she attempted to change the subject. "How about you? Any prenuptial jitters?"

"Of course not," Blythe answered quickly. A bit too quickly, Lily thought. "Why would you ask?" Despite the denial, Blythe's tone was lacking in its usual assertiveness.

Lily shrugged. "No reason. I was just making conversation."

Seeming no more eager than Lily to have her statements challenged this morning, Blythe held out a cup. "I made you a cup of herbal tea. I seem to recall reading it's best to watch caffeine during pregnancy, but if you'd rather have coffee—"

"Tea's perfect," Lily assured her.

Blythe had always been an expert on so many things. The fact that this intelligent woman who'd graduated with a degree in economics from Brown was invariably cast as a luscious sex goddess was definite proof that Hollywood was a land of images and illusion.

Lily sat down at the table and glanced at the faded newspaper photos spread across the glass top of the wicker table.

One portrayed a stunningly beautiful woman, posed in the glamour style of the 1930s lying on a satin chaise. She was wearing a clingy white silk negligee trimmed in marabou feathers that hugged her body like a lover's caress. Her hair was a thick sable cloud around her face, her lips were full and dark.

Although those voluptuous lips were curved in a staged, provocative smile, Lily imagined she viewed sorrow in the gypsy dark eyes. The caption beneath the photo revealed that the sultry love scenes in Alexandra Romanov's latest film, *Lady Reckless*, had earned Xanadu Studios yet another fine from the Hays commission.

A second clipping, from *Motion Picture News*, showed Alexandra on the dance floor, in the arms of a ruggedly handsome man clad in a white dinner jacket. They made a stunning couple. They were also obviously very much in love. The emotion in the woman's eyes, as she smiled up at the man, was not the sadness of the earlier photo, but uncensored desire. This time the caption proclaimed Alexandra Romanov and Western writer Patrick Reardon to be the most fascinating newlyweds on the planet.

"They look so much in love," Lily mused out loud.

"Don't they?" Blythe sighed. "That was taken shortly after they eloped. I've often thought if I ever found a man who looked at me the way Patrick is looking at Alexandra, I'd marry him on the spot."

Since Blythe actually *was* getting married tomorrow, Lily couldn't help wondering if Alan Sturgess, Blythe's intended husband, fitted the profile.

Yet a third newspaper clipping, which, along with the accompanying story, took up the entire front page above the fold, depicted Patrick Reardon alone. His eyes were as dark and bleak as a tomb. The banner headline running across the top of the newspaper copy was brief and to the point: "Reardon Executed."

"So, how's the project coming?"

Lily knew, from shared telephone conversations over the past few months, that Blythe had formed her own production company and parlayed her box office fame into a multipicture deal with Xanadu Studios. The tragic, star-crossed story of Alexandra Romanov and Patrick Reardon was to be the company's first feature film.

The brutal death of the glamorous, tempestuous 1930s sex symbol at the hands of her tough-talking, hard-drinking, hot-tempered husband had been the scandal of the decade. More than sixty years later, it remained Hollywood's most infamous murder.

"Not as well as I'd like." For the next ten minutes, Blythe filled Lily in on the frustrating lack of information about the actress in the studio archives.

"After all," Blythe complained, "Alexandra Romanov's films were the primary source of income for Xanadu Studios in those days. If I didn't know better, I'd think
the woman was a Russian spy and the CIA has classified
her files."

For a business reputed to be built on creativity, Lily
knew, from all the stories Blythe and Cait told about Hollywood, that it was money that kept the magical, mysti-
cal Dream Machine oiled and running.

"Considering the box office gate during Alexandra's
heyday, you'd think Xanadu would have erected a shrine
to her," she mused.

"You would, wouldn't you? But things are looking up,"
Blythe revealed with a burst of the characteristic can-do
attitude Lily had always admired and sometimes envied.
"I hired a private investigator to dig into the story and he
managed to find the makeup artist who worked on all of
Alexandra's films when she was under contract to Xanadu."

"How will that help?"

"Most performers tell their makeup people everything."

"Like women and their hairdressers."

"Exactly. Anyway, I really thought Gage—Gage Remington, he's the detective—had solved our problems, but
it turned out that the woman's away on a cruise. She's due
to return next week."

"While you're in Hawaii. On your honeymoon." Lily
knew Blythe didn't believe Patrick was guilty of killing his
wife. She also figured that after sixty years, the murder
mystery could wait a few more weeks.

"That won't be a problem. Gage has promised to call me
as soon as he talks with her."

"Won't Alan object to having his honeymoon interrupted for business?" she asked carefully. After meeting the bridegroom for the first time last night, Lily had the impression that the renowned Beverly Hills plastic surgeon didn't much approve of anything concerning the film industry.

"He probably won't be thrilled," Blythe admitted with obvious reluctance. "But he understands that my work is important to me."

Her words were one thing, the way the light in her eyes had dimmed suggested another.

"There's something I've been meaning to ask you," Blythe said on a hesitant tone that told Lily she was treading carefully into dangerous conversation territory.

"What's that?"

"I realize that you have a lovely home in Connecticut, but I was thinking..." She dragged her hands through her hair. "Lord, I've been practicing this scene for the past two weeks, you'd think I'd have it down pat."

"What scene?"

Blythe took a deep breath. "Okay, here goes. Every time we've talked on the phone lately, you've seemed depressed, which of course, is understandable, what with Junior's death and all . . ."

When her voice drifted off again, Lily wondered what Blythe would say if she knew that when she'd first heard of her husband's fatal accident, her first reaction had been one of pure relief.

"It's been difficult." That much was definitely true.

"Of course it has." Blythe reached out and covered Lily's hand with her own. "Which is why I want you to consider moving in here."

"Here?" Lily glanced around the cheery sunroom. "With you and Alan?" When Lily had expressed surprise that

Blythe and her fiancé were not currently living together, Blythe had explained that Alan, always conscious of appearances, worried that cohabitating with an actress known for her sexy roles would cast him in a bad light with the powerful hospital governing board.

Blythe had gone on to reveal that after a great deal of negotiation, Alan had reluctantly agreed to sell his own home in Pacific Palisades and move in here after the wedding.

"It's an enormous house. We'd hardly know you were here."

"What about after the baby's born?"

"We can turn the dressing room adjoining your guest bedroom into a nursery. Unless you think it's too small, then—"

"It's certainly not too small."

Indeed, the two rooms together were larger than most of the cramped apartments Lily had been looking at. Lily tried to imagine changing diapers on the exquisite Louis Quinze dresser in her guest room and failed.

"It's just that I hadn't given any thought to moving."

Now that *was* a lie. Ever since being served those horrid papers by her in-laws, she'd considered running away on an almost daily basis.

But not to Los Angeles. Rio de Janeiro, perhaps. Or some remote tropical island where the Van Cortlandts would never find her. Or, more importantly, where they'd never find her child.

"Cait and I both feel you should be close to friends at this difficult time in your life," Blythe said, pressing her case.

The idea, as out of the blue as it was, proved wonderfully tempting. "I'll think about it."

"Good." Blythe nodded her satisfaction, seeming as if the matter had already been settled.

The next day, the wedding began as yet another sun-spangled California in paradise. The scent from the brightly colored, blossom-laden bushes drifted upward on the warm air, filling the bedroom of Blythe's home with their sweet perfume.

Exhausted from another restless night, during which she'd suffered vivid nightmares reenacting her near drowning, Lily stood in the open doorway leading out onto the second floor bedroom balcony and gazed down at the scene below.

A formally dressed harpist was entertaining the small gathering of family and guests seated on rented white satin-seated chairs. Beneath a white arbor emblazoned with scarlet roses, the groom waited for his bride.

Lily sighed and tamped down a twinge of envy. Despite Beverly Hills being a long way—both geographically and socially—from Iowa, her best friend's ceremony was remarkably like the one she'd wanted for herself.

Although she definitely would have left out the helicopters, which, hired by reporters from the tabloid press, were hovering noisily overhead.

When James Carter Van Cortlandt Jr. had proposed Lily had been ecstatic, looking forward to the wedding she'd dreamed of since childhood.

She'd be married in Hastings, Iowa, in the Methodist church where she'd attended Sunday school, and where her parents still sang in the choir every Sunday morning. Guests would be the same friends and family who always gathered together to celebrate the good times and help each other survive the bad.

People like Jake Iverson, down at Iverson's Feed and Grain, who never complained when the bill got a little high or the payment came a little late. Or Iris Brown, who, when Lily's mother was confined to bed with pneumonia during the long hard winter Lily turned ten, dropped by every night with a casserole.

Or Shelley Mosley and Julie Havir, librarians from the county bookmobile, who had, over the years, not only supplied Lily with books to feed her hungry mind, but had helped her fill out the mountain of paperwork that had earned her a work-study scholarship to the prestigious Ivy League college.

Her attendants would, of course, be her best friends— Caitlin Carrigan and Blythe Fielding.

Frustrated by what he considered Lily's outdated insistence on going to her marriage bed a virgin, Junior hadn't cared where they were married, or who was in attendance when they exchanged their vows. The only thing he was interested in was getting the legal paperwork signed.

Lily's wedding plans were immediately overruled by her future in-laws.

"My dear Lily," Madeline Van Cortlandt had sniffed, "although I have no wish to interfere in what should be the bride's family's role, I feel obliged to point out that there is no way our friends and Mr. Van Cortlandt's numerous business acquaintances could possibly attend such a distant, rural event."

Although tempted to point out that this was supposed to be a marriage, not a merger, loyalty toward her fiancé had Lily holding her tongue. He couldn't help it, Lily had told herself, if Madeline was a snob. Only too late would she learn that Junior was even worse than his mother.

Lily had caved in. It was better this way, she'd assured Cait and Blythe, who'd counseled her to have the wedding she wanted. There was no way her parents could afford the elaborate ceremony the Van Cortlandts were expecting.

And although she'd always considered herself an imaginative person, Lily could not envision Junior's patrician parents toasting the wedding couple with Mrs. Warner's cranberry-ginger ale punch in a town grange hall festooned with white crepe paper and silver cardboard bells for the occasion.

Which was why she and Junior had ended up exchanging vows to a packed crowd in the Gothic Revival style St. Thomas Episcopal church on Fifth Avenue.

Her subsequent marriage—beginning with her husband getting drunk at the reception and ending with Junior's violent death in a car crash six months ago—had proven a disaster.

"You're so lucky," Lily murmured to Blythe who'd come to stand beside her and was looking down into the garden.

"Lucky?"

"My Grandmother Padgett always said, 'Happy is the bride the sun shines on.'"

Her words reminded the three friends that it had been raining cats and dogs the day she'd married the scion to all those banking millions.

"As nice a thought as that is, Lily," Cait drawled, "I'm not sure it counts out here. Since the sun shines just about every day. And Lord knows, California's divorce rate isn't anything to brag about."

"I suppose you're right." Lily ran her palms down the front of her pleated maternity dress and felt her baby turn yet another somersault.

Only two more months and she'd be able to hold her child in her arms. The thought, which she clung to like a drowning woman might cling to a piece of driftwood, had been all that had kept her from falling apart since she'd been served those hateful papers drawn up by the Van Cortlandts' attorneys.

"It's just a saying, after all," Lily murmured, trying to shake off the suffocating cloud that settled over her whenever she thought of those cold legal words.

"But a nice thought," Blythe said in an attempt to bring a smile to Lily's pale lips.

Lily knew Cait and Blythe were worried about her. She'd seen the looks they had exchanged when they first viewed her coming off the plane from New York.

Determined not to ruin Blythe's wedding with her own looming problems, Lily had shrugged off their concern, blaming jet lag and the overly active gymnast who'd taken up residence inside her body for her depression.

But she was so worried—strike that, she corrected—she was so *frightened*, it was all she could do not to break into tears. Or scream. She suspected either response would be better than continuing this lie she'd been living for so long.

Lily frowned up at the circling helicopters that were drowning out the harpist. Unsurprisingly, the secret had gotten out. Lily had the sinking feeling that they were all her fault.

Although she didn't believe Mac Sullivan would have called the tabloids, she would certainly not put such behavior past their taxi driver.

Cait was glaring at the copters as well. "I should get my shotgun out of my patrol car and shoot those damn things down."

"Terrific," Blythe said dryly. "All this city needs is a news story about a vigilante cop. Complete with video." She frowned as she watched the wind from the rotors whip the scarlet roses from the trellis. "Not that it isn't tempting," she admitted.

"You are looking," Cait muttered darkly, "at one more reason I try to avoid this business." Helicopters had disrupted her actress mother's last two weddings.

As Blythe and Cait continued to observe the scene, Lily left the doorway and crossed the lush carpeting to the dresser, where she checked her reflection in the mirror.

Never having been a vain person, Lily had never compared her appearance to that of the two women who'd started out as her roommates their freshman year at college and had become her closest friends.

After all, Cait's exquisite beauty was a fortunate genetic inheritance from her famous actress mother and screenwriter father. No mortal woman could possibly hope to compete with Cait Carrigan's mass of fiery hair, flawless complexion and wide, expressive emerald eyes. As for Blythe, Lily had witnessed grown men run into walls while staring at her friend's lushly curved body.

Lacking Cait's flamboyant coloring and Blythe's sultry dark looks, Lily had always relied on her personality. She'd always possessed an enormous energy that had belied the fragility of her pale blond looks. An energy more than a few young men back home in Iowa, and during those house mixers at college, had found appealing.

But now, frowning at her image in the beveled glass, she decided that Mac Sullivan's interest yesterday had undoubtedly been nothing more than an act of pity on his part.

No man could possibly find her the slightest bit attractive. Even discounting the weight she'd gained during the seven months of her pregnancy, her pallor and the dark circles below her tired, listless eyes revealed her recent lack of sleep. Her depression was etched into brackets on either side of her full pale lips, making her look older than her twenty-five years.

"I look like something the cat dragged in," she complained, tucking in a few loose hairs that had escaped the French braid.

"You look lovely," Blythe insisted. "Have you thought any more about what I suggested yesterday?"

"About staying here with you and Alan?"

"It would be wonderful having you close by," Cait weighed in. "I hate the idea of you having your baby all alone, with just those snooty old Van Cortlandts standing by."

"I'm thinking about it," Lily said.

Before her two best friends could pressure her further, the anniversary clock on Blythe's dresser chimed the hour, signaling it was time for the trio to go downstairs.

The moment brought back a jolting sense of déjà vu. Lily's blood turned cold as she remembered, in vivid detail, that last instant—stilled like a freeze frame forever in her mind—before she walked down the aisle, when she'd experienced a foreboding so strong it had made her knees weak.

She watched Blythe take a deep breath meant to calm.

"There's still time to change your mind," Cait advised.

"Don't be silly." Blythe threw back her bare shoulders. "I'm not going to disappoint all those people down there."

Lily exchanged a puzzled, concerned look with Cait, whose bleak expression told her that they were thinking the same thing.

Ever since Lily's arrival Cait had been hinting that the upcoming wedding was not exactly a match made in heaven. And although Lily had admittedly been too wrapped up in her own worries to pay close attention, now, seeing Blythe appear less than ecstatic about the upcoming ceremony made her share Cait's concerns.

"Better to disappoint a few friends than spend the rest of your life regretting what you did," Lily advised.

It was the same thing her father had told her before she'd walked down that long aisle in St. Thomas's. How many times since that fateful day had she wished she'd taken his advice!

But then, Lily amended with that strong sense of midwestern practicality that had always served her well, if she hadn't married Junior, she wouldn't be about to have his baby. A child she had absolutely no intention of giving up.

Blythe shook her head and managed a weak laugh that drew Lily's wandering mind back to their conversation. "The two of you are overreacting to a simple case of prewedding jitters." She scooped up her bouquet from the bed and marched out the door.

Exchanging a worried look, Cait and Lily followed.

3

FEELING LESS than graceful and certain that she was wad-
dling like some pregnant duck, Lily slowly walked down
the white satin runner that was a twin of the one used at
her own wedding and felt as if every eye in the garden was
focused on her swollen belly.

Although her obviously pregnant condition drew a few
murmurs—and a faint, disapproving frown from the
groom—most of the people gathered for Blythe's wedding smiled.

When she reached the rose-covered arbor, Lily turned
and watched as Cait took her turn. Lily knew that the
dark-haired man, seated in the front row between Blythe's
parents and Natalie Landis, Cait's movie star mother, was
Sloan Wyndham, the man Cait was currently involved
with. It was also the man Blythe had hired to write the
screenplay for her Alexandra Romanov project.

Cait had pointed him out from the upstairs balcony and
now, as she watched Sloan watching Cait approach on her
confident, long-legged stride, the love emblazoned across
his handsome face assured Lily that one of them, anyway,
had chosen well.

When the harpist viewed Blythe's appearance in the arbor, she broke into the wedding march. The assembled
guests all turned to view the bride. Blythe's dress was elegant, yet simple by Beverly Hills standards—a sleek, off-
the-shoulder, short-sleeved ivory crepe tunic over a long
slender skirt.

To Lily's surprise, Blythe stopped midway down the runner. Seemingly oblivious to the gathered guests, she looked straight into the face of a dark-haired man who was staring at her.

A curious murmur drifted over the garden. Although she felt like a voyeur, intruding on some private moment, Lily could not drag her own eyes away from Blythe and the stranger,

"Lord," Cait, who was standing beside Lily, murmured, "Gage and Blythe. Who would have thunk it?" Her low tone was laced with both surprise and pleasure.

"Gage?" Lily murmured back. "That's the detective who's supposed to prove that Patrick Reardon didn't kill his wife?" When Blythe had mentioned him yesterday, Lily's imagination had conjured up a cigar-smoking former cop in a rumpled trench coat.

"That's him," Cait confirmed. "And whether Reardon turns out to be guilty or innocent, it looks as if Gage could be Blythe's Mr. Right."

Cait's surprising answer had Lily glancing toward the groom. Dr. Alan Sturgess had gone rigid. His eyes, directed toward his bride, who still hadn't moved, were icy lasers.

"Are you saying Blythe's really in love with this detective?"

"She hasn't said a thing about it," Cait admitted. "But hope springs eternal. Remember the scene in *The Graduate*, where Dustin Hoffman runs off with Katherine Ross?"

"Of course, but..." Lily turned and stared at Cait. "Surely you don't think Blythe would actually run away from her own wedding and leave her groom standing at the altar?"

"We can only hope."

"She'd never do it." Lily knew Blythe was incapable of such behavior. "She doesn't have it in her to publicly embarrass anyone that way."

"You're probably right." This time Cait lifted her eyes toward the delphinium blue sky. "What we need now is a little divine intervention." Her words were cut off by a low, deepening rumble, like an approaching freight train.

"Oh, hell," Cait muttered. "Talk about your direct response."

A moment later, a massive, upward jolt beneath her feet knocked Lily to her knees. The violently shaking ground disoriented her, making her feel as if she'd suddenly dived back beneath the sea. The horrible, grinding noise of earth and stone reminded her of those giant pneumatic drills that broke up sidewalks.

Closing her eyes tightly, Lily began desperately reciting prayers learned in childhood. All around her, pandemonium broke loose in a thunderous cacophony. The white satin-seated chairs bucked wedding guests in all directions, causing them to land on top of one another, their screams of alarm unable to be heard over the deafening roar of the bucking, trembling, grinding earth.

Having grown up in tornado alley, Lily knew firsthand how violent nature could be. Yet nothing had prepared her for the enormity of a California earthquake. She pressed her palms tight against her stomach where her baby was behaving as violently as the trembling earth beneath her.

Making things even more terrifying was the way it seemed as if the earth would never top shaking. Time took on an eerie, slow-motion feel. Shattered glass from the windows was raining down like an Iowa ice storm.

Finally, the swaying and rocking began to diminish. The ear-splitting sound of the earth's crust being broken quieted. Miraculously, Death released its grip.

Still shaken, Lily opened her eyes and cringed, viewing destruction all around her.

She saw Blythe, lying beneath Gage Remington amidst a pile of broken chairs. Nearby, Alan Sturgess, who'd been thrown against the arbor, appeared hopelessly tangled amidst the thorny rose bush.

The swimming pool, which only seconds earlier had been a tranquil lagoon set like a jewel surrounded by fragrant flowers, had slid down the steep hillside.

Amazingly, Cait had landed nearly ten feet away. She was lying beneath a pair of white-framed French doors that had burst out of the house. Sloan was attempting to make his way toward her when he was knocked down by a second aftershock.

Refusing to believe that she could have survived yesterday's near drowning only to die in an earthquake hours later, Lily curled up in a ball and desperately waited for the terror to end.

San Francisco, California

IT WAS RAINING. Since that was not an unusual occasion for the Bay area, the inclement weather failed to darken Connor's mood. After all, he had a great deal to celebrate. Not only was he the proud new owner of one of America's oldest and most revered movie studios, he had just destroyed his lawyer on the handball court.

After leaving the racquet club, the two men were sitting at the bar in the San Francisco Brewery Company— where Jack Dempsey once worked as a bouncer—drinking Scotch and toasting the recent successes of the man that the *Wall Street Journal* had recently called a financial wunderkind with a Midas touch who didn't realize the go-go eighties were over.

After six months of intense, secret negotiations, the papers had been signed yesterday. Xanadu Studios had been purchased, lock, stock and sound stage, by C. S. Mackay Enterprises.

"By the way," Connor said, "I want you to drop the lawsuit against the Van Cortlandt estate."

"Why the hell would you want to do that? Have you forgotten the man's unethical activities cost you nearly a million dollars?"

Connor's jaw hardened at the memory. "I never forget anything."

"Then why—"

"Let's just say it's personal, and let it go at that."

His lawyer gave him a long look, but receiving only a steady, implacable one in return, finally shrugged. "It's your money." Knowing that there was no point in arguing when Connor Mackay had made up his mind, he changed the subject.

"So, how does it feel to join the ranks of Sam Goldwyn and Darryl Zanuck? You *are* going to set your friends up with some of those gorgeous Hollywood actresses, aren't you?"

"I bought a studio, not a brothel," Connor pointed out good-naturedly. "I'm afraid you'll just have to struggle along, winning women with your good looks, money and charm. As for how it feels, it's not half bad."

Connor grinned like a fraternity boy who'd just pulled off a major prank. "Not bad at all. In fact, I've been thinking about moving to Tinseltown and becoming a hands-on movie mogul. Maybe I'll even start with Blythe Fielding's new project."

The mention of the sultry actress had him thinking again of her friend, Lily Van Cortlandt. As he'd been doing a lot since their dramatic meeting yesterday morning.

"Although I can definitely understand the appeal of working with the delectable Ms. Fielding, as your attorney, I'd advise against that idea," Aaron drawled. "Failure tends to drive investors back into the woodwork."

"What makes you think I'd be a failure?" Although his statement had been made in jest, Connor took his friend's warning as a challenge. From the time he was five years old and his cousin Dylan had double-dog-dared him to swallow a night crawler, Connor had never been able to back away from a challenge. "It just so happens that I like movies."

That was definitely an understatement. The truth was, he loved the medium. Connor's taste in films, like everything else about him, could not be pinned down. A regular patron at the kind of small art theaters specializing in obscure foreign films with subtitles, he was just as likely to be seen working his way through a jumbo box of popcorn while watching an action-adventure thriller at the mall multiplex.

As for movies made in what had become known as the Glory Days of Hollywood, his private collection of 1930s films had recently been donated to Berkeley's film library. Indeed, before buying the studio, Connor had been meeting with a syndicated group of theater owners thinking to establish a national chain. The day that deal had fallen through, Walter Stern III providentially arrived at his office, metaphorical hat in hand.

"A great many people like movies," the attorney said. "But that doesn't mean they're capable of running a studio."

"I didn't know all that much about race horses before I bought one, either."

"The difference is that where that horse—and the subsequent breeding farm—were concerned, you were smart enough to leave the training to an expert. The same way you did with that rafting company."

After a twenty-one-day trip riding the Colorado rapids in the Grand Canyon, Connor had purchased half interest in the rafting company run by two former Chicago litigators, allowing them to expand their venture into Idaho, Oregon and Wyoming.

"Your problem, Connor," Aaron Morrison alleged, "is that the entire idea of movies is to appeal to the masses."

"So?"

"So, in order to make successful movies it's necessary to understand middle-class values and interests. Which would be extremely difficult for you to do, having been born with a silver spoon in your mouth, a platinum American Express card in one hand and a fistful of stock coupons in the other."

Although he'd been hearing similar allegations all his life, for some reason, coming from a man who was not only his lawyer, but his best friend, the insinuation stung. Especially since it reminded him all too clearly of what Lily had said about never getting involved with rich men.

"In the first place, the project Blythe Fielding is trying to get off the ground is a story about Alexandra Romanov. Who was definitely not the girl next door," he said. "Neither was Patrick Reardon the boy next door. From what I've read, during that brief time they were married—"

"Before he murdered her," Aaron broke in.

Something about the accusation irked Connor. "During that brief time they were married," he repeated firmly, "Alexandra and Patrick were Hollywood's most glamorous couple. So, if the studio does end up producing their story, it won't exactly be a treatise on middle-class values.

"And may I also take this opportunity to point out that just because I was born with a silver spoon in my mouth doesn't mean that I haven't learned to feed myself." Although his voice was calm, his dark brown eyes were not.

"Really, Con," Aaron complained as he signaled the bartender for another Scotch, "there's no crime in being rich, so don't be so damn sensitive."

Having descended from one of San Francisco's Irish Big Four families—known as The Silver Kings—the Mackays had always prided themselves in living up to the generously philanthropic standards set by their ancestors.

Unlike the city's other Big Four—the so-called Railroad Barons, who defined the unsavory robber baron category of the era—the Silver Kings were not so much unscrupulous as they were lucky.

From the time their famed bonanza, The Comstock Lode, was discovered in 1859, to the mine's closure ten years later, the vein of shiny ore poured $500 million worth of silver into the pockets of partners James C. Flood, William S. O'Brian, James Graham Fair and John William Mackay.

Unwilling to rest on some distant ancestor's laurels, most members of succeeding generations worked hard, contributed greatly to the family fortune and continued their generosity to a variety of social causes.

"I could give up all my money," Connor claimed recklessly. "Right now and never miss it."

"That's easy to say. Since it's a moot point."

Connor could not believe that this man he'd known all his life, the same man who'd been his best friend for thirty-one years, could actually think him so shallow that he couldn't separate his money from his character.

"I'll make you a little wager," he said as the impulsive idea suddenly occurred to him. "I have thirty days before

I'm scheduled to show up at the studio to announce takeover plans. I'll bet, during that month, I can successfully
pass myself off as a common, ordinary working man."

"You've got to be kidding," Aaron said on a laugh.

"Not at all." The more he thought about the idea, the
more Con liked it.

"What are the terms?"

"If I lose, I'll throw a party at the studio. And invite you
and ten people of your choice, along with every actor and
actress who's ever been under contract to Xanadu."

"Including Blythe Fielding?" The attorney's tone suggested that he expected Connor to lose the wager. It also
suggested that he found the idea of meeting the sultry, dark
sex symbol more than a little appealing.

"She'll be at the top of my list," Connor promised. He
folded his arms across the front of his chest. "So, how
about it?"

"What about if you win? What will you want me to put
up?"

"I intend to win," Connor said matter-of-factly. "And
when I do, I'll expect you to write a five-thousand dollar
check to a charity of my choice."

Aaron Morrison only hesitated for a moment. A smug
look settled on his face. "You're on. But we need to set
down some ground rules."

Ten minutes later, they had compiled a detailed list when
the bartender turned up the volume on the television.
Glancing up, Connor asked, "What's up?"

"L.A. just had an earthquake."

"That's not so unusual." Having grown up in San Francisco, he'd come to view tremblers as a fact of life.

"The early pictures they're showing sure don't look
good," the bartender muttered. "Ted Koppel just said this
might be the Big One."

Beverly Hills

MERCIFULLY, the trembling, rocking earth was still. The deafening crescendo of rock being broken had been replaced by a cacophony of thousands of car and home alarms going off all over the city.

Disoriented, her blood pounding in her ears, Lily lay in the middle of a huge puddle of water, staring in disbelief at the destruction around her. Every window in Blythe's magnificent home had burst out of its frame.

Two of the chimneys were rubble and the third looked decidedly iffy. There were cracks in the walls of the house the width of breadsticks. The pool house had been knocked off its foundation.

Concerned for her friends, Lily was relieved when she saw that Sloan had managed to get the French doors off Cait, who was conscious enough to fling her arms around his neck and kiss him. Not far from the embracing couple, Gage was helping Blythe to her feet.

When Lily struggled to stand up, black spots swam in front of her eyes. A sharp pain attacked her lower back like an arrow hitting a bull's-eye. Her knees, already shaking from adrenaline, gave way, causing her legs to fold beneath her.

As she sank back into the pool of water, Lily surrendered to the darkness.

When she felt herself beginning to float toward consciousness again, she was being lifted into a pair of strong arms and carried across the rubble that had only minutes earlier been an exquisite garden in full bloom.

"The phone lines are out from the quake," Blythe, who was hurrying along beside her explained. "And we can't get through on anyone's cellular to call an ambulance.

Gage came up with the idea of using the Rolls to take you and Cait to the hospital."

As Lily looked into the calm silvery blue eyes of the man deftly weaving his way toward the teeming throng of wedding guests, she suddenly recalled the way Blythe and Gage had been staring at one another just before the quake had hit.

"Thank you."

He smiled and through the fog clouding her mind, Lily noticed that it held considerable charm. "Just part of the job."

"Gage used to be a policeman," Blythe explained as the driver rushed to open the door to the Rolls-Royce limousine hired for the wedding party. Cait and Sloan had followed behind them; Cait was holding Sloan's handkerchief to a cut on her temple.

After they all were inside, with Lily lying on one of the glove soft, white leather seats, Blythe remembered her manners. "Lily Van Cortlandt, Gage Remington."

Another fact registered in Lily's mind. "You're a detective."

"Private, these days."

Lily nodded, her earlier fear being replaced by resolve. Her in-laws had hired a detective to dig into her past. What if she was able to unearth a few family skeletons in the illustrious Van Cortlandts' closet?

"How are you feeling?" Blythe asked, her concern obvious.

"I had a pain in my lower back. But it's gone now."

"No cramps?"

"No."

"Or bleeding?"

"I don't think so."

"I'm sure you and the baby will both be all right."

"Of course you will," Cait said firmly. The once snowy handkerchief was turning pink; her face was unnaturally pale.

"I *know* we will," Lily said. She'd already lost too much. The man she'd thought she loved, her marriage, her home and most of her money. Lily was not about to lose her child.

Which brought her back to the Van Cortlandts' lawsuit. Ignoring Blythe's murmured protest, she sat up and gave Gage a direct look.

"I'd like to hire you. If you're not too expensive."

He did not appear at all surprised by her request. "I'm sure we could work something out." When he gave her another smile, even warmer than the first, Lily realized exactly how this man might prove a devastating temptation to a less than enthusiastic bride.

"What on earth do you need a private detective for?" Cait asked, her interest piqued.

"It's a long story."

"You need your rest," Blythe insisted. "Why don't you and Gage talk after we have the emergency room doctor check you and the baby out?"

Surprise at Lily's statement, along with a glimmer of curiosity, flickered across Blythe's face. Lily knew she was dying to ask. She also knew that unlike Cait, who never hesitated speaking her mind, Blythe wouldn't press for details.

Although she was worried that she'd already waited too long to begin her defense, Lily also realized that this was neither the time nor the place to discuss her upcoming custody battle.

"I'm not going anywhere," Gage offered gently. "Besides, we're almost there and I don't think a hospital emergency room is exactly conducive to constructive conversation."

Despite the seriousness of the situation, Lily managed a smile. "You must be a mind reader."

"Only sometimes." His easygoing smile faded as he looked over at Blythe. Once again, their gazes locked. The air surrounding them grew electric.

They'd reached the hospital, but neither Gage nor Blythe appeared to notice. Just when Lily was certain the limo was going to burst into flames, the driver stopped in front of the doors to the emergency room.

"I can walk," Lily protested as Gage scooped her up again, as easily as if she were a feather.

"Of course you can," he said agreeably. "But there's no point in taking chances, is there?"

Having no answer to that, Lily didn't argue.

The emergency room was chaotic, but the staff, trained in disaster response, kept things moving amazingly smoothly, despite the aftershocks that were keeping everyone's nerves on edge.

"Your friend appears to have suffered nothing more than a bit of a shock," the doctor, whose musical accent suggested Indian roots, assured Blythe after Lily had been examined. "But it appears you've hurt yourself."

Blythe followed the physician's gaze to her sleeve. Noticing the dark stain for the first time, she was belatedly aware of a burning in her left arm. "I'm sure it's nothing," she said.

"I believe that's for the doctor to decide," Gage, who was standing beside Blythe, said. His voice, while low, sounded too much like an order for Blythe's liking.

"I'm fine," she insisted.

"Why don't you let me be the judge of that?" The doctor took a pair of surgical scissors from the pocket of her white lab coat and slit the seam of the wedding dress's sleeve. "You have a sliver of glass imbedded in your arm," she announced. "We'll have to remove it. And clean the wound."

"Can't we do it later?" Still worried about Lily, Blythe wanted to get her settled into a bed. She glanced around at the bedlam spilling out onto the parking lot. "Surely you have more serious cases to examine."

The doctor pursed her lips and made a decision. "Promise you won't let her leave without having this cared for," she said to Gage.

As he felt Blythe seething beside him, Gage grinned. "You've got yourself a deal, Doc."

Within minutes, Lily was admitted for observation and hooked up to a fetal monitor. Gage and Blythe were with her when a very frustrated Cait came storming into the double room.

"Dammit, Gage," she complained, "would you please explain to Sloan about a cop's duty!"

"The idiot's insisting on going to work," Sloan, who was on Cait's heels, ground out.

Cait turned on him, her hands on her hips. There was a huge tear in her short skirt, revealing a ruffled lace slip. "You'd think a man who earned his living writing screenplays would chose his words more carefully. Is that any way to talk to the woman you profess to love? If you dare call me an idiot after we're married—"

"Married?" Blythe interrupted, her pleased gaze going back and forth between the arguing couple. "Really?"

"If I can keep her alive long enough to get her to the altar." Sloan's irritation was not visibly eased by Blythe's obvious pleasure at the news. "It was bad enough having her nearly killed when she went undercover to capture that surfer rapist. This latest stunt proves she's crazy."

It was his turn to seek support from Gage. "You used to be her partner. Tell her that going out on the street in the middle of a disaster zone, when she's suffered a head injury, is not only stupid, it's dangerous."

Gage's silver-blue eyes moved judiciously over Cait's face, taking in her uncharacteristically pale complexion and the row of black thread at her temple. "You've had stitches."

She folded her arms over the bodice of her bridesmaid's dress. "Not that many."

"Nine," Sloan abruptly corrected. "And why don't you tell him about the doctor's warning about a possible concussion?"

"He's just being overly cautious because he's worried about a malpractice suit. I'm not going to hang around here, lying in bed, when the city needs every cop it can get out on the street."

"Not cops in danger of passing out and driving their black-and-white into a crowd of civilians," Gage corrected in the same calm, reasonable tone Cait had watched him use to defuse a dangerous situation back in the days when they'd been working the mean streets of South Central L.A. together.

"There's not a commander on the force who'd let you out on the street ten minutes after getting stitched up for a head injury, Carrigan. And you know it."

Her frustrated breath ruffled her bangs. "So I'll work dispatch."

"The hell you will," Sloan corrected with a flare of his own temper. "You're going home. To bed."

"That's what all this is about, of course," Cait said, addressing Lily for the first time since bursting into the room. "The man can't keep his hands off me."

Cait's fiery temper had defused as quickly as it had flared. Lily had seen it happen countless times during their college years together. "Lucky you."

She smiled up at Sloan. "Looks as if Cait's finally met her match. Don't let her run over you."

Ignoring Cait's muttered curse, Sloan put aside his own irritation and grinned. "I'm going to give it my best shot." His smile moved to his eyes, which were laced with concern for Cait. And also, Lily noticed, for her. "How are *you* feeling?"

"The doctor assured us you were going to be fine," Cait said quickly, as if embarrassed not to have inquired earlier.

"I am. I just want to get out of here."

"Tomorrow," Blythe promised. "The doctor wants to keep you overnight. Just in case."

Although Lily definitely wasn't looking forward to the prospect of spending the night in the hospital, surrounded by strangers, neither did she want to do anything to jeopardize her baby.

"I suppose that makes sense," she agreed reluctantly.

"Now *there's* an intelligent woman," Sloan said to Cait. "Why can't you be more like your friend?"

"Now we're back to calling me an idiot?"

"Never an idiot." He slipped his arm around her waist, drew her to his side, and pressed his lips tenderly against the row of dark stitches. "Just overly dedicated at times."

"It's my job."

"Exactly," Gage pointed out what it had taken him so long to learn himself. "Police work is only your job, Carrigan. Not your life."

"Putting things into neat little compartments may work for you, Gage Remington," Cait repeated what she'd said so many times during the four years they'd been partners.

"But I'm not like you. I could never walk away from The Job.

"I'm a cop all the way to the bone. It's what I do. And who I am. I couldn't separate the two if I wanted to, which I don't. And right now, I'm going back to work."

Breaking away from Sloan, she turned and started marching on her long-legged, determined stride toward the door. She was nearly there when she stopped, put her hand to her head, then slowly folded to the floor.

While Sloan cursed and rushed to her side, Gage nodded, appearing satisfied and not the slightest bit concerned.

"Well," he drawled, "I guess that settles that argument."

Within minutes, a protesting Cait had been admitted into the empty bed beside Lily.

The nurse returned, informing Blythe that the emergency room staff was now ready to treat her wound. Muttering about the entire event being a monumental waste of time, not to mention valuable personnel, Blythe reluctantly obliged. Not because she necessarily wanted to, but because she had the suspicion that if she refused again, Gage would literally scoop her up and carry her into the emergency room for treatment, just as he had Lily.

"You're not coming with me," she said, correctly perceiving his intentions. "I'm more than capable of having a little cut cleaned without you hovering over me like some overprotective German shepherd police dog."

Once a cop, always a cop, she figured. It was obvious that Gage Remington could not resist bossing people around. Once this adventure was over, Blythe was going to remind him that she was the one who'd hired him. She should be the one giving the orders.

Gage shrugged. "Whatever you want." His casual tone belied the frustration in his gaze.

Lily watched Gage watch Blythe leave. Although he was doing his best to hide it, she could see the unwilling desire in his intriguing eyes.

"So, where's the bridegroom?" she asked.

Gage shrugged again. He'd dispensed with his suit jacket and tie. His white shirt was open at the collar, the sleeves rolled up, revealing strong, darkly tanned forearms.

"He said something about having to get to a hospital across town where he's on staff."

"Makes sense to me." Lily knew that plastic surgeons did far more than face lifts and tummy tucks. If the quake was as bad as it had seemed in Blythe's garden, there would undoubtedly be a great many people needing Alan Sturgess's services.

Having noticed Gage's protective attitude toward Blythe, Lily was tempted to probe into their relationship, when another aftershock, which had the lights flickering overhead, precluded any questions.

4

ALTHOUGH HE WAS no stranger to earthquakes, Connor could hardly believe the destruction that greeted him after arriving in Los Angeles.

From the air, the scene had resembled a huge, albeit flimsy, monopoly board that some giant had carelessly toppled, strewing houses and hotels everywhere. But as bad as the City of Angels had appeared from the executive jet, down on the ground, things were even worse.

As he inched along in the rental car, contributing to the massive traffic jam that threatened to paralyze the city into one enormous grid-locked parking lot, Con felt as if he'd landed in the middle of a scene from *The Road Warrior*.

The flooded streets were filled with rubble, gas leaks were burning, and everywhere you looked people were milling around, shaken and disoriented.

He drove to Blythe Fielding's home immediately after landing at Orange County's John Wayne Airport. If he'd been worried about Lily before arriving at the house, one look at the destruction, along with the news that Lily and a cop named Cait Carrigan had been taken to the hospital, made Connor's blood run cold.

When the phone lines to local hospitals proved jammed, he tried calling police stations in search of news concerning officer Carrigan. Unsurprisingly, those lines rang busy as well.

Finally, just when he thought he was going to go stark raving mad with worry, he lucked out. He got through to the Hollywood division, where an obviously harried press officer revealed that officer Carrigan had been taken to the University of California Medical Center.

When he finally got through to the hospital, Connor had absolutely no qualms about telling the operator he was calling on official police business. After a few clicks and a horrible moment when he thought he'd been disconnected, the call was transferred to officer Carrigan's room.

"Hello?" an unfamiliar feminine voice answered.

"I'm looking for Caitlin Carrigan," Connor said.

"Who's this?" the voice inquired with a suddenly sharp edge that confirmed he was talking to a cop. Connor opened his mouth to answer when he remembered his real name would mean nothing to Lily Van Cortlandt. Realizing he was going to have to explain eventually, he chose the easy route.

"Mac Sullivan."

"The white knight?"

"Excuse me?"

"You're the guy who pulled Lily out of the drink yesterday, right?"

"That's me." He wasn't surprised Lily had mentioned him. After all, she would have had to have offered some reason for returning to Blythe Fielding's home with wet clothes and kelp hanging from her hair.

"Are you calling from San Francisco?" Cait asked.

"No. I'm here in L.A."

There was a moment's pause. "I thought Lily said you were on your way home."

"I was. Now I'm back."

Another pregnant pause. "Would Lily have anything to do with your rapid turnaround?"

"She's part of the reason," Connor admitted. "May I speak with her?"

"Just a minute." Connor heard her talking with someone, presumably, Lily. Seconds later, Cait was back on the phone. "I'm sorry, but Lily's not here right now. She was taken down to—uh—X ray."

He didn't know what kind of cop Caitlin Carrigan was, but she was a lousy liar. Realizing that Lily had put her up to the blatant falsehood, he tamped down his frustration and concentrated on his concern.

"How is she?"

"The doctor says she's fine."

"And the baby?"

"Is also fine."

"Then why the X rays?"

"It's only a precaution." There was another pause, a heartbeat longer than the others. "You're not married or anything are you, Mac Sullivan?"

He heard a voice in the background and suspected Lily was protesting Cait's pointed inquiries.

"No, I'm not married. Or anything."

"How interesting."

Connor wished she'd just talk her friend into taking his call. "Look, why don't I come by the hospital?"

"That's not a good idea," she said quickly. "I'll tell her you called. Do you have a number where you can be reached? In case she wants to get back to you?"

Not at all happy with the suggestion—he was certain it would be a very cold day in Los Angeles before Lily returned his call—Connor nevertheless gave her the number for the cellular phone he was using in the rental car.

"I'll pass it on," Cait assured him, as if reading his own negative thoughts. "But I can't promise anything."

That said, she hung up.

Connor cursed and was trying to decide what the hell to do next when the phone rang.

"Lily?"

"It's Cait. Look, I'm going to have to make this quick, because I'm using a pay phone down the hall and I already misused my badge to cut into a very long line. Do you have a piece of paper and pen handy?"

"Sure."

"Write this down." She gave him an address he recognized as being in the Wilshire district. "Cait's going to be moving into my apartment building now that Blythe's house is wrecked. Do you think you could drop by tomorrow?"

"What time?"

"Afternoon? Around two or three?"

"I'll be there."

"Good." He heard the raised voices of complaint in the background and sensed her preparing to hang up.

"How is Lily?" he asked quickly. "Really?"

"She's had a rough time lately. But I think you may be just what the doctor ordered."

Her laugh, right before she broke off the connection, was rich and warm and utterly feminine. But as appealing as he found it, Connor realized that it did not affect him nearly as strongly as Lily Van Cortlandt's soft smile.

"Tomorrow," Connor promised.

That matter settled, he turned his attention to his other reason for being in Los Angeles.

Xanadu Studios, located in the San Fernando Valley, between Warner Brothers and the larger studio-theme park acreage of Universal, had once been ranch land. Intending to use the sprawling property solely to film westerns, Walter Stern had bought the land more than sixty years ago.

When commuting between the valley and downtown became a hassle, his son, Walter Stern II sold off the land that housed the downtown Hollywood studio and moved the entire operation to the San Fernando Valley.

Only two days ago, Connor had made the drive from LAX to Xanadu in thirty minutes; today, forced onto surface streets along with millions of other drivers, it took two hours to make the one-way trip.

By the time he exited Ventura Boulevard, turning onto Xanadu Drive, Connor was hot and frustrated and rethinking his decision of having bought a damn movie studio in the first place.

But then the elaborate wrought iron gates—which were, he saw with a rush of cooling relief, still standing—came into view and he experienced an adolescent rush of excitement. This legendary dream factory actually belonged to him.

As requested, Walter Stern III, grandson of the studio's founder, was waiting for him in his office. Despite the fact that he'd been the one to initiate the sale of the longtime family-held studio, Stern did not appear at all pleased to see the new owner.

"You didn't have to fly all the way down here," he said with a patently false smile that didn't begin to touch his cold blue eyes. "I had everything under control."

Although under normal conditions he preferred keeping the original management team in place, especially during the initial takeover, Connor couldn't discount the fact that the problems Xanadu was facing had been largely brought about by Stern's mismanagement in the first place.

Connor's answering smile was as feigned as Stern's as he shook hands. "As it turns out, I had to come to town, anyway."

Steely blue eyes narrowed. "I thought we'd agreed we wouldn't make the announcement for a month."

"We did." Hell. This wasn't going to work, Connor thought with an inward sigh. At first he'd tried to discount his unease regarding the movie mogul. But today, the vibes were proving stronger than ever. Although Stern had never actually done anything to precipitate such intuitive feelings, for some reason Connor had yet to discern, he didn't like the man.

"My initial reason for coming back to L.A. had nothing to do with Xanadu. But after what's happened, I thought I should stop by and survey the damage."

"Remarkably, given the severity of the quake, it's not that bad," Stern assured him. "Mostly some flooding from burst water pipes. Oh, and we lost the backdrops for the Paladin western, but they're easily replaced."

"That's good news." Connor certainly hadn't been looking forward to starting out his newest venture in a flood of red ink. "I was hoping you'd have time to give me a tour."

It was an order. Softly spoken, but couched in stone. A muscle clenched in Stern's cheek, but he managed an obliging smile. "That's precisely what I was going to suggest."

As he walked back down the hallway, lined with photos of the studio's stars, and cases displaying the studio's myriad Oscars, it crossed Connor's mind that as vast as Xanadu was, there would never be room for both him and Stern.

And since he had no intention of leaving, his only choice was to ease the former owner out. Hopefully, the parting would be amiable. If not, Connor reminded himself that he'd never been one to back down from a fight.

After examining the studio property and buildings, Connor was on his way to his suite in the tower at the Century Plaza when he realized the detour had put him in Cait Carrigan's neighborhood.

Struck with a sudden urge to drive by the property, as he pulled up in front of the Mediterranean pink apartment house, a For Rent sign immediately caught his eye.

He cut the engine and spent a long time studying the building that had obviously once been a single-family dwelling. The apartment house boasted turquoise trim and lacy iron grillwork on the windows and balconies on the upper floors. A turret, while not in keeping with its Spanish style, somehow seemed to fit.

The hotel suite waiting for him in Century City boasted a private balcony, wet bar and refrigerator, three phones and an all-marble bathroom with a separate tub and shower, oversize bath towels and terry robe. There were plants, including a live tree in the living room, and most appealing was the marble Jacuzzi, which, on one memorable occasion, he'd shared with a sexy Bank of America vice president.

The hotel was the height of luxury, the service unsurpassed. It was also, he admitted, far beyond the grasp of a common, ordinary man. Suddenly mindful of the bet that the earthquake had temporarily expunged from his mind, Connor studied the building for another long moment.

Then, acting on impulse as he so often did, he climbed out of the car and walked up the sidewalk.

The plaque on the outside wall by the arched front doorway read Bachelor Arms. Below the plaque, someone had scratched *Believe the legend.*

Connor found the manager's apartment and rang the bell. Once. Twice. A third time. Frustrated, he turned to leave just as a young woman exited the next-door apartment.

"Hi! Are you looking for Ken?" she asked with a friendly smile.

"I am if he's the manager."

"He had to go out of town for a couple weeks. Great timing, isn't it? What with the earthquake? Luckily we didn't have any major damage.

"Anyway, he claimed to have some kind of family emergency." She ran a hand through thick brown, naturally highlighted hair. "Personally, I think he's off rendezvousing with the mother ship."

"The mother ship?"

Brown eyes danced with humor. "Ken's nice enough, but he's a little spooky." She glanced around as if seeking out spies. "I believe that there's a very good chance he's a pod person. But Bobbie-Sue—she's my very best friend?—says I'm just overreacting from preparing for my audition.

"I'm up for a supporting role in a remake of *I Was a Teenage Werewolf*," she confided. "Xanadu's making it. My agent says I'm a shoo-in. Next week I'm actually reading for Walter Stern himself. Can you believe it?"

"I didn't realize studio heads conducted auditions personally," he said with studied casualness.

"To tell you the truth, neither did I." She flashed him a dazzling smile. "But Roger—that's my agent, Roger Kendall, he used to be with William Morris, before he opened his own agency?—assures me that it's not that unusual. For Xanadu."

Rosy lips designed to inspire masculine fantasies turned downward. "Bobbie-Sue says Mister Stern's just trying to get into my pants. So does Eddie.

"Eddie has a script under consideration at Xanadu and says that Stern's a lecherous rat, but of course he hasn't been treated very well there, so he's probably prejudiced."

She leaned back against the wall, crossed her arms over her bouncy, cheerleader breasts and eyed Connor with good-natured interest. "What do you think?"

What did he think? Connor thought that if this perky southern belle routine wasn't a contrived act, the lady was too naive to survive long in Tinseltown. He also thought he'd better keep an eye on Stern until the takeover was concluded.

"I think it never hurts to be careful," he said.

She sighed and dragged her pink-tipped fingers through her long straight hair again. "You're probably right. Cait warned me of that same thing, and since she's a cop, not to mention both her parents being in the business, well, she knows how ugly this town can be, beneath the glitter. If you get my drift."

Connor managed a nod, opened his mouth to agree, but she was off and running again. "But Mister Stern seemed so nice when I met him at that party last week."

"I'm sure he's sincerely interested in your talent," Connor assured her, saying what he suspected she wanted to hear.

Brenda Muir rewarded him with a dazzling smile designed to bring the average man to his knees. Having never considered himself an average man, Connor had no interest in getting involved with this perky steel magnolia.

Experience had taught him that actresses were riddled with insecurities that tended to also make them frighteningly egocentric. Connor preferred to keep his relationships with the opposite sex light and uncomplicated.

Which made him wonder why it was he was suddenly interested in a woman who could only complicate his life.

"I told Bobbie-Sue that Mister Stern was only interested in my acting ability," Brenda revealed. "After all, I did graduate from Yale Drama School. I've even played Nora, in Ibsen's *A Doll's House*?"

"I'll bet you brought the house down," Connor answered obligingly.

She laughed. "Lord, you are good for a girl's ego." Those merry brown eyes took another, slower, tour of him, obviously approving of what they saw. "I'm Brenda, by the way. And I do hope you're planning to move in."

"I'm thinking about it." He slipped his hands into his pockets and rocked back on his heels. "So, if the pod person's out of town, who's showing the apartment?"

"That'd be Jill."

"Terrific. Where can I find her?"

"You can't." Her lips curved into a self-deprecating grimace. "I forgot, she's in San Diego, attending a design show. She's an interior decorator. You should see what she did for my apartment. She gave the key to Bobbie-Sue, who at the moment is working next door."

"Next door?" He glanced at the neighboring apartment door.

"At Flynn's, on the corner. It's a neighborhood bar, kind of like 'Cheers'?" As it had before, her voice went up a little on the end of the sentence, turning it into a question. "It's where people in the neighborhood all hang out. Eddie's the bartender. And Bobbie-Sue works there part-time while she looks for a job."

"Acting?"

Her grin was quick and bright and appealing. "What else? In this town?"

What else indeed? Connor thought. He wondered what would happen if Brenda, Bobbie-Sue and Eddie the bartending screenwriter knew that the new owner of Xanadu Studios was considering moving into their midst.

Actually, Connor considered as he walked beside Brenda, who'd insisted on showing him the way personally, the idea, which had begun as a spur-of-the-moment impulse, wasn't all that bad.

Both Brenda and Eddie were involved in dealings with Xanadu.

What better way to find out exactly how Xanadu's executives treated the people they worked with than to actually live among them, listening to them report their personal experiences?

Connor decided he was experiencing yet another stroke of the famed Mackay luck.

If he hadn't been stopped by the beach yesterday, if he hadn't met Lily Van Cortlandt, he'd never have spoken with Cait Carrigan, which meant that he'd never have known Bachelor Arms—and its eclectic mix of tenants— even existed.

As he entered Flynn's, Connor decided that fate was indeed a wonderful thing.

"Fate," Gage said with a slow shake of his head, "can be a damned fickle thing."

Standing beside him, dressed in the green scrubs she'd borrowed from the hospital to replace the torn, muddied and bloodstained wedding dress, Blythe stared at the empty slip where the sloop that served as Gage Remington's home-office had been docked only yesterday. Amazingly, and unluckily for Gage, the sleek yachts on either side of his sloop appeared undamaged.

"I can't believe it's gone," she said.

Although Gage had wanted to take Blythe directly back to her home, she'd insisted on having the limousine driver take them out to Marina del Rey first. In truth, she was not all that eager to face what she feared would be waiting for her at home.

"Sunk." Gage swore and dragged his hand down his face. When he took it away, he cast his eyes skyward. "I know I haven't exactly been an altar boy, but if you'd wanted to get my attention, Lord, couldn't you have just knocked down a mast or something?"

Blythe thought it said something about Gage's character that he could find grim humor in a situation like this. Although some inner voice told her that touching this man could lead to trouble, she placed a hand on his arm.

"Surely it was insured?" She felt the muscle tense beneath her fingers.

"I *think* earthquakes are covered under my boat policy. But even if it is, a check from the insurance company isn't going to recover the files from the bottom of the harbor."

Blythe's heart sank even lower than Gage's lovely boat. "Including the files on Alexandra?"

"Including those." Then he laughed, because crying over what he couldn't do anything about was not Gage Remington's style. "But don't worry. It'll take some time, but they can be duplicated."

He watched the relief flood into her remarkable dark eyes and although he knew it was dangerous, he thought about kissing her, of pressing his mouth hard against hers, of holding her lush curves against him until they both were burning with the need for more.

Unaware of his heated thoughts, Blythe was thinking about their situations. It looked as if they'd both been relegated to the ranks of the newly homeless. From the destruction she'd witnessed before leaving for the hospital, there was a very good chance her lovely house would be condemned. It would be months before it was inhabitable again.

"What are you going to do in the meantime?" she asked.

Unaware that he was even doing it, Gage reached out and twisted a sable curl around his finger. Beneath the antiseptic smell of the hospital lingering in her hair, he detected the sensual scent of tropical flowers. "About what?"

Did he know what he could do to her? Blythe wondered. With only a look? An innocent touch? Her mouth was dry, her heart was beating rapidly. She licked her suddenly parched lips and realized she'd made a big mistake as she watched flames rise in his intense gaze.

"About where you're going to live." She managed to sound coherent but Blythe knew she was in big, big trouble when it took no effort at all to imagine his mouth seizing her lips.

Forgetting caution, forgetting that she belonged to another man, forgetting everything but the need to touch, Gage could not resist tangling his hands in her hair. "I'll do what you're probably going to do. Move into a hotel. Or maybe an apartment."

The wooden dock, reacting to yet another tremor, swayed beneath their feet. When she instinctively lifted her hands to his shoulders to brace herself, his free hand, just as instinctively, settled on her hip to steady her.

"It's just a small aftershock," he assured her on a voice roughened not with fear but desire. "There's no need to worry."

"I'm not." Her voice, soft and hesitant, sounded unfamiliar to her own ears. She wasn't worried, Blythe assured herself. Not about any earthquakes, anyway. "Not really."

His fingers tightened. "You're trembling."

"I know."

"Do you always tremble when a man touches you?"

She swallowed and forced herself not to drag her eyes away from his steady, unnerving gaze. "No." There was no point in lying. "I think this is a first."

The dock stopped swaying. But Blythe's heart was still thrumming painfully as she stood there, looking up at him, knowing she and Gage were both remembering how, as she'd walked down the aisle, their minds had inexplicably tangled, exchanging words neither of them had even known they'd been thinking.

You can't do this, his stormy eyes had told her.

I have to, hers had answered back.

You don't have to do anything, his countered on a flare of passion. *But leave with me. Now.*

I can't.

You can. He'd held her wary gaze to his with the sheer strength of his will. *I'll help you.*

They hadn't said a word out loud. But it hadn't been necessary. And although they'd never exchanged a single personal word since the day she'd hired him to unearth information about Alexandra Romanov and Patrick Reardon, Blythe had found herself unreasonably tempted to take Gage up on his outrageous demand.

Then, blessedly, it had happened.

The massive, upward jolt beneath her feet had hurled Blythe into Gage. They were both thrown violently to the ground. The strange, suspended moment had been shattered.

But not forgotten.

"You have dirt on your face," Gage said now. The hand that had tangled in her hair brushed against her cheek. It was a rough hand, calluses on calluses, that felt like the finest grade sandpaper against her suddenly hot skin.

"It probably happened when I landed in the flower bed."

"Probably." His fingers slowly trailed down the slanted line of her cheekbone, around her jaw, creating an ache that went all the way to the bone.

"I can still feel you," he said on a rough voice that thrilled Blythe far too much for safety. "Lying beneath me, all soft and warm." His hand moved down her neck, his thumb measuring the rapid jump of her pulse in the hollow of her throat. "You felt good, Blythe." *Too good,* a vague little voice of conscience reminded him.

"You shouldn't talk to me that way."

She fisted her hand against the front of the dress shirt that had, only hours earlier, been as pristinely white as her wedding gown and was now filthy. Whether she was fighting herself or him, Blythe did not know.

"Do you know," he murmured, ignoring the soft protest they both knew she did not mean, "that I've been wanting to kiss you since that first day you showed up at my boat." Gage realized he should be heartsick about the loss of the sloop. Formerly owned by a drug kingpin, he'd bought the boat for a just barely affordable price at DEA auction. It was mortgaged to the top of its mast and even if the insurance company did pay up, it wouldn't be nearly enough to cover his losses.

But how could he complain when the same quake that had scuttled his home had also thrown Blythe Fielding into his arms?

"I didn't know you felt that way," she lied, recalling all too well that stunning moment on his deck, when their eyes had first met and they'd both suffered that same strange jolt of recognition.

"Of course you did." His tone, as he called her on the blatant falsehood, was as reasonable as it had been when he'd been arguing with Cait earlier in the hospital. But it was ever so much warmer. More intimate. "I've been working for you for what, a month now?"

"Twenty-eight days." Heaven help her, she'd actually counted. And not just to keep track of daily expense payments.

"That long." His lips quirked. "I've always been known for my patience," Gage said, telling Blythe nothing she didn't already know. She'd come to admire the way he methodically combed through dusty old file clippings and microfiche archives. "But the way I see it, twenty-eight days thinking about a kiss is about twenty-seven days too long."

The pull was irresistible. With only the faintest touch, he drew her closer, until they were touching—thighs to chests. "I think it's past time I got this out of my system." His dark head slowly lowered. "Out of our systems."

5

BLYTHE TRIED TO THINK of all the reasons why she should back away, now, while she still could. First and foremost being that she was engaged to another man. That if the earthquake hadn't happened, she'd be on her way to Maui right now.

But even knowing that what she was about to allow was terribly wrong, Blythe stayed where she was, watching, transfixed, as Gage's firmly cut mouth lowered toward hers.

He nipped lightly at her lips. Once. Twice. Then again, giving her ample time to back away. She should stop him, Blythe told herself as a slow, sweet ache curled through her. She would stop him. Soon.

Her mouth was everything he'd known it would be. Warm. Generous. And so painfully sweet. Gage cupped his fingers on the back of her neck, holding her to the kiss he had no right to steal. But there was no need. Blythe's soft lips parted on a tiny moan of pleasure, inviting him to deepen this wicked, wonderful kiss that both knew to be as inevitable as it was forbidden.

They kept their eyes open—him watching her, her watching him. His pale blue eyes were fierce, revealing a dark, dangerous side of him Blythe had never seen before. Hers were wide, so dark as to be nearly black, and laced with a reckless passion that, although she'd never— ever—felt it before, seemed strangely familiar.

Her breathing quickened. Her hands crept up his chest to link together around his neck. Displaying that inordinate patience she'd come to expect, he began driving her slowly crazy.

His lips teased. Tantalized. Tormented. She'd kill him for this, Blythe vowed as she finally allowed her eyelids to drift shut. If she didn't die first from unrequited need.

"Dammit," she complained shakily, wanting—needing!—him to relieve the tension that was building up inside her like a pressure cooker, "if you're going to kiss me, do it."

She pressed closer. Her breasts flattened against his chest. "Stop torturing me this way."

Gage needed no second invitation. As her mouth turned hot and avid, his turned rough and ruthless, taking what he wanted, then demanding more.

His lips crushed hers, his teeth nipped at the tender skin, his greedy tongue invaded the dark recesses of her mouth in a way that had her meeting him, primal demand for primal demand, heat for heat. A host of wildly primitive urges were beating hotly in her bloodstream, causing her to dive headlong into the kiss.

Although she'd never been a publicly demonstrative person, if Gage wanted to drag her down onto the floating wooden dock and take her right here, right now, Blythe knew that she would not do a single thing to stop him.

As his heart pounded painfully in his chest, as heat pooled thickly, achingly in his loins, Gage wondered what it was about Blythe Fielding that stimulated such mindless, uncontrollable passion.

He wanted to rip those ugly green hospital scrubs off her, he wanted to touch, to taste, every fragrant inch of her hot, moist flesh. He wanted to bury himself deep inside her and take them both to some dark, secret place where reason disintegrated and passion ruled.

Gage knew it was dangerous to want a woman like he wanted Blythe. He knew it was madness to *need* a woman like he needed Blythe. The problem was, he had never feared danger. And, if this was madness, Gage would take it over reason any day.

Another aftershock sent the dock swaying. Caught up in the power and fury of the shared kiss, neither Gage nor Blythe noticed. She opened her mouth and tasted his hunger. It thrilled her. She opened her heart and felt his need. It almost made her weep.

As his hands moved roughly up and down her sides, from her shoulders to her thighs, caressing her full curves, gripping her hips as if wanting to pull her inside him, Gage realized she was everything he'd been dreaming of, without having realized he'd been dreaming.

As he feasted hungrily on the sweetness of her parted lips, he knew she was everything he'd been hungering for, without having realized he was starving. She was all he'd ever craved.

And she was taken.

Although it was the hardest thing he'd ever done, Gage dragged his mouth from hers.

She murmured a faint, incoherent protest.

This time they both felt the unstable earth beneath the marina tremble. If Gage's legs hadn't already been widely braced—the better to pull her into his heat—if he hadn't been holding onto her, they'd have fallen into the water.

Which might, Gage considered with a saving burst of self-directed humor, cool them off. Or, more likely, set the harbor boiling. He reluctantly broke away, more for his sake than hers.

Shaken by internal forces even more powerful than the mightily external ones that were wreaking havoc on the city, Blythe stared up at Gage. What had she been thinking of, passionately kissing another man while her fiancé labored to put broken bodies back together again?

Gage viewed the guilt flooding into her eyes and realized he'd been the one to put it there. "I didn't force that kiss on you." He cursed inwardly as he heard how stupidly defensive he'd sounded.

Although she was inexplicably near tears, Blythe used every ounce of her acting skills to portray a calm she was a very long way from feeling.

"I didn't say you did," she reminded him with a toss of her dark head.

"I'm not going to apologize."

Blythe welcomed the burst of irritation caused by the way he was rejecting what they'd just shared. "I wouldn't think of asking you to." She lifted her chin. "It's been an extremely emotional day. I suppose it's inevitable for people under such stress to behave irrationally."

The way he was standing there, inches away, staring down at her, was making her increasingly uneasy. She wondered if he'd used that strong silent treatment on criminals back in the days when he'd been a cop. It was definitely proving more effective than bright lights and rubber hoses.

"I mean—" she, who'd never babbled in her life, began to talk too much and too fast, "—during your days on the police force, you undoubtedly observed similar behavior. During the riots, perhaps. Or the wildfires."

She combed her hand through her tangled hair in a gesture he'd come to recognize as nerves. "And surely during the '94 earthquakes you witnessed several—"

"Blythe." He caught her hand as it took another sweep through the dark waves. "I get the point."

"Oh."

Watching the color rise in those incredible, knife-edged cheekbones, Gage found himself struck with a need to comfort. "Things have changed."

She knew he was not talking about the earthquake. "Not really," she protested weakly. "As I was saying—"

Before she could finish what they both knew would be a lie, his head swooped down and he gave her a brief, hard kiss that rocked her.

"Things have changed," he repeated. "And we're going to have to deal with those changes."

"I can't." Although she'd always been known for her composure, the complaint came out on a ragged wail. "Not now. My house has been reduced to a pile of bricks and broken glass and twisted water lines. I have to deal with the insurance company, not to mention having my film to worry about, and I'm going to have to plan another wedding—"

This time he cut her off with a dark finger against her mouth. Gage didn't want to hear about her marriage. He didn't want to think of her going off to Hawaii, drinking Mai Tais decorated with little paper umbrellas and making love on the sand beside a tropical lagoon with that stuffed shirt doctor.

What the hell did she see in the guy, anyway? Gage wondered, even as he reminded himself that it was none of his business.

"Don't worry. I'm not going to interfere with all your important plans. Not from Florida."

"Florida?"

"I told you, I have a lead on Alexandra." Was that alarm he viewed in those expressive dark eyes? Regret? "Remember?"

"Oh. Of course."

His gaze skimmed over her, remembering all too painfully, how good, how right, she'd felt in his arms. Because he wanted to take her to the nearest hotel and finish this, Gage decided the time had come to distance himself from his dangerous attraction. For now.

"We'd better get over to your house," he said in that level, no-nonsense tone favored by cops all over the world. "And see if we can salvage any of your things. Before the inspectors slap a red tag on the place."

"What about you?" At least Blythe had her clothing. And her cosmetics. And hopefully, in the wall safe behind the Robert Reid impressionist painting of a young woman in a field of flowers, what few papers she had concerning Alexandra and Patrick remained safe and sound. Gage had lost everything he owned.

"It's only stuff," he said with a careless shrug.

She tried to imagine how it must feel to be bereft of everything but the clothes on your back and failed.

"At least let me give you an advance," she protested. "So you can replace some of the more important items right away," she explained at his suddenly sharp look. "You'll need things for your trip. Clothes, toiletries, spending money..."

He stared at her for a long time, giving Blythe the impression that he was silently comparing their lifestyles. He was.

Prepared for some acid comment, or worse yet, an accusation about the spending habits of wealthy women, he surprised her yet again by throwing back his head and laughing.

"I hadn't realized I'd said anything so humorous," she said stiffly, feeling like a fool even as she didn't exactly understand why.

Gage couldn't decide which Blythe Fielding he was more attracted to. The lush, hot-blooded siren who could match him passion for passion, or this cool, remote ice goddess whose acute business mind belied a body built for sin.

"You didn't." Knowing it was a mistake, he caught her stiff chin between his fingers and held it to a soft, strangely tender kiss that sent streamers of silvery heat through her. "Not really. It's just that you're kind of cute when you're being earnest."

No one had called her cute since her body had turned into that of a woman the summer of her thirteenth year. Even as she tried to be insulted by his chauvinistic behavior, Blythe found her lips curving upward.

"Should I be insulted?"

"Hey, I may just be an ex-cop turned P.I., but I do know enough not to insult a client." The smile reached his eyes. He traced her lips with his index finger. "For the record, I don't keep my money—what little there is of it—in a shoe box beneath my bunk, Blythe.

"Except for fifty dollars in my wallet, the rest of my cash is sitting in an interest-bearing checking account at the Marina del Rey Citibank branch."

"I'm glad," she said, meaning it.

"I know," he said, encouraged that she cared.

Because he could not be this close to her without touching her, Gage reached out and linked their fingers together. And although it didn't make a lick of sense, the easy, casual gesture felt both right and familiar.

"This isn't right," she murmured, looking down at their hands and revealing that once again they were sharing the same thought.

"Perhaps not." His jaw firmed, the smile vanished from his eyes, turning them as hard as pale blue stones. "But right or wrong, when I get back from Florida, we're going to finish it."

Still shaken by the passion that the reckless kiss had ignited, and confused by these feelings Gage Remington inspired, Blythe refused to answer.

Extricating her hand from his larger, darker one, she returned to the waiting limo.

As the car inched along, searching out detours on the drive to Beverly Hills, Blythe turned her attention out the window and reminded herself firmly that she was an engaged woman. These strange, unruly feelings for Gage would pass, Blythe assured herself. She would make them pass.

"I CAN'T BELIEVE I'm doing this."

In the past twenty-four hours, not only had she experienced her first earthquake, she'd also further shaken up her life by allowing Blythe and Cait to talk her into cashing in her return ticket. Not that it took all that much convincing.

"Name one good reason to go back east," Cait argued after she and Lily exited her cherry red Mustang in front of Bachelor Arms. Blythe, who'd driven her own car from the hospital, had arrived seconds earlier and was waiting for them on the sidewalk. "And Bloomingdale's doesn't count."

"Since I don't have any money to go shopping, Bloomingdale's is a moot point." Although she'd tried to keep her problems to herself, under Cait's relentless interrogation, her tale of woe had finally come spilling out of her last night.

"I didn't like those snooty old Van Cortlandts when I first met them at your wedding rehearsal," Cait muttered.

"They're only doing what they think is best," Lily said, trying to find some reason for her in-laws' behavior.

"You're overdoing the Mary Sunshine routine, Lily," Blythe surprised both women by snapping. "If the Van Cortlandts were so damn good at raising a child, their son wouldn't have turned out to have been a philandering son of a bitch and you wouldn't be in this mess in the first place."

Both Lily and Cait stared at Blythe, surprised by her uncharacteristic flash of anger. She was usually far more tolerant.

"It's not that I don't agree with you, because I do," Cait said. "But you sound as if you got up on the wrong side of the bed this morning, Blythe."

"In order to have gotten up on the wrong side of the bed, I would have had to have been there in the first place." Blythe shook her head with lingering frustration. "I was up most of the night making lists for the insurance company." That wasn't exactly the entire truth. Blythe had returned home to discover that her house did, as she'd feared, have a red condemned tag on the front door. Fortunately, Gage, who knew the officers securing the area, had talked them into letting her inside to retrieve a few essential items.

From there, Blythe had checked into a bungalow at the famed Château Marmont Hotel. The hotel had been offering privacy to its celebrity guests since 1929; the fact that Alexandra Romanov had stayed there when she'd first arrived in Hollywood made it even more appealing.

What Blythe wasn't prepared to admit was that she'd spent much of her first night in the bungalow staring down at the yellow legal pad, thinking of Gage Remington, remembering that strange moment when she'd been walking down the aisle, and as impossible as it seemed, their minds had melded.

As disturbing as that memory had proven, she'd also spent far too many dark lonely hours, reliving, in agonizing detail, that wicked, wonderful kiss.

And if all that hadn't been upsetting enough, during those predawn hours when she'd actually managed to drift off, Blythe had been plagued by terrifying nightmares about Alexandra Romanov's life. And death.

She shook off a faint, lingering depression. "Moving here, away from those horrible Van Cortlandts, where you have people to support you is the right thing to do, Lily," she repeated what she'd said when Cait had first told her of their friend's untenable situation. "I only wish you could stay with me at the house."

"I'm sure I'm going to love it here at Bachelor Arms," Lily said. It was mostly true. Anything was better than returning to Connecticut, where, as hard as she'd tried, for Junior's sake, she had never felt at home.

"I do feel a little guilty about Gage," she admitted as the three women headed up the brick walk. "If I hadn't put him on the spot that way, asking him to take my case, he probably wouldn't have felt obliged to hire me."

Gage had offered her a job answering his phone and typing up reports. Until he returned from Florida and found some place to live, his calls would be transferred to Lily's number.

"Don't be a dope. He needed the help," Cait insisted.

"I can vouch for that," Blythe agreed. "I can't count the times I've had to leave messages on his answering machine. Or his beeper."

After promising Lily that he'd begin investigating the Van Cortlandts as soon as he returned, Gage had left Los

Angeles late last night. Blythe told herself that she wouldn't miss him and wondered when she'd become such a liar.

"Jill said the apartment she had in mind for you is on the first floor," Cait announced as they entered the pink building. "You're going to love it; it has the most darling little garden in back. I can just see the baby, lying in her buggy in the sunshine."

The image was a pleasant one. Oh yes, Lily thought with a burst of optimism, things were definitely looking up.

They stopped by Jill's office. The sexy blond interior designer, whose knockout curves and highlighted blond hair reminded Lily of Linda Evans from her "Dynasty" days, greeted her prospective tenant with genuine warmth.

"I know how difficult it is to start over," she said as she retrieved the key from a Queen Anne desk in her living room. "I don't know if Cait's filled you in on everyone, but I recently moved here after my divorce." Her smile was bright and friendly. "You're going to discover that L.A. is a perfect place to reinvent yourself."

Her words struck a responsive chord deep inside Lily. "That's exactly what I intend to do."

During her soul-searching walk on the beach the other day, she'd belatedly realized she'd been drifting for months. Since before her pregnancy. Before Junior's death. It was time to regain control. Time to make a new life. For herself, as well as her baby.

"There was a bit of earthquake damage," Jill revealed. "And unfortunately, Ken—he's the man who takes care of the building—is out of town."

"How much damage was there?" Cait asked, suddenly concerned about her own apartment.

"Don't worry, your place is fine," Jill assured her quickly. "In fact, we were pretty lucky. Most of the units managed to escape unscathed. Your apartment," she said to Lily, "has a cracked window that needs replacing and some bookshelves came unfastened from the wall. But I've hired a temporary handyman to fill in while Ken's away."

"That was fast work." Even having figured out that Jill was incredibly motivated and organized, Cait was still impressed with the speed with which she'd located a replacement.

"Actually, I was out of town yesterday," Jill revealed. "I didn't get back until this morning."

"Then who—"

"Brenda found him. He's another new tenant."

"Brenda?" Cait arched a brow. Brenda Muir was bubbly, beautiful and enthusiastic. And terribly naive.

"I know." Jill's laughter revealed Cait was not alone in her concern for what type of handyman the would-be actress may have hired. "I was worried, too. But I gave him the tour, and from what I could tell, he knows his way around a hammer."

She handed Lily the key. "After Cait called about you needing a place to stay, I told him to start with your apartment."

The arched door was ajar. As Lily approached with Blythe and Cait, they heard a rich baritone belting out a rendition of Roy Orbison's "Pretty Woman."

"He certainly has a nice voice," Blythe offered.

"He's enthusiastic anyway," Cait allowed. "I hope he can hammer as well as he sings." Despite Jill's assurance, she still didn't quite trust Brenda's hiring acumen.

The first thing Lily saw as she entered the apartment was a man clad solely in a pair of faded, raggedy cutoff shorts and a pair of sneakers. Even as she told herself that such an instantaneous sexual response was unseemly in a woman only two short months away from motherhood, the sight of those sinewy muscles rippling in the man's bare back as he pounded nails into the wall nearly took her breath away.

"I knew it," Cait muttered darkly as she came up behind Lily. "Brenda's gone and hired a Chippendale dancer as a handyman."

The scathing tone captured his attention. He turned toward them, looking ridiculously macho with that large, wood-handled hammer in his hand and the leather tool belt slung low on his hip.

"Well, well," he drawled as his gaze went directly to Lily's startled face. "If it isn't the pregnant mermaid. Talk about your small worlds."

Lily couldn't believe her eyes. "Mac?"

Cait's surprised gaze went from Connor's handsome face to Lily's astonished one and back again. "Mac?" Good Lord, she thought, no wonder Lily was so willing to stay in California! "*You're* Lily's white knight?"

Lily's soft unpainted, utterly kissable mouth had parted in an appealing O of surprise. Even as he told himself that the woman he'd pulled out of the surf represented more complications than any sane man would want, Connor was drawn to the soft color that was drifting into her cheeks. "That's me. In the flesh."

And so much flesh, Lily considered weakly. His chest was tanned to the color of the Honduras mahogany breakfront that her great-great-grandmother Padgett had insisted on hauling along in that covered wagon from Vermont to Iowa so many years ago. The same one each generation of Padgetts had cherished, the one that she'd inherited when her parents had died, the one that Junior had refused to have in their house. The one currently in a Lock-and-Store in Hastings.

A light sheen of perspiration glistened on that muscular chest, drawing her attention to the arrowing of hair that disappeared below the waistband of his faded cutoffs.

A flurry of emotions—none of them safe or comfortable—rushed through her. "I thought you said you'd come to town on business," she said, when she finally found her voice.

"I did." That was the absolute truth.

Lily had learned the hard way not to trust a smooth smile and dancing eyes. "And now you're a handyman?" Her arched brow echoed her skeptical tone.

Having already lied to her about his name, Connor hedged. "Don't tell me you have something against honest work."

"Of course not." There was something wrong here. Something Lily couldn't put her finger on. "It's just that most rich men of my acquaintance don't earn their living hanging up shelving."

Having been personally acquainted with one particular rich man Lily Van Cortlandt had known too well, Connor didn't blame her for her distrust. "You're the one who said I was rich," he reminded her with a negligent shrug that drew her unwilling attention to his broad shoulders.

The part of her that wanted to believe him considered that he was too fit, too tan, for a man who spent his days behind a desk in some high-rise office tower. Another more cynical part she'd developed after her marriage found him too smooth, too comfortable with himself to be a mere carpenter.

"You didn't correct me," she said.

"I didn't get the chance. You closed the door on me before I could effectively argue my case."

He didn't talk like any handyman Lily had ever met, either. She turned back to Cait and Blythe.

"We need to talk." If Mac Sullivan was going to be working at Bachelor Arms, there was no way she could live here.

He was too attractive.

Too tempting.

Too male.

"It's nearly lunchtime," Cait said. "We could go next door to Flynn's."

"Anywhere is fine with me." Without giving Connor a second glance, Lily turned and walked out of the apartment.

"What in the world was that all about?" Jill asked.

Cait had a feeling she knew exactly what was bothering Lily. "Hormones," she said instead. "You know how temperamental pregnant women are."

Obviously unconvinced, Jill glanced over at Connor, who only gave her a bland, innocent look in response. "Well, is she going to take the apartment or not? With so many buildings being damaged in the quake, a lot of people are going to be looking for new places to live. I can't hold it forever."

"She'll take it," Cait said quickly.

Now that she'd seen Mac Sullivan, and discovered he'd be living here as well, Cait was more determined than ever to have Lily move into Bachelor Arms.

As a cop, Cait prided herself on her instincts. Often her life depended on her well-honed intuition. And although she shared Lily's obvious suspicion that this was not the man's usual line of work, she also sensed that he was a good man. A decent man. Not to mention being about the

sexiest thing—not counting Sloan, of course—that she'd
seen in ages.

She and Blythe had been hoping for something to take
Lily's mind off her troubles. And providentially, here he
was.

"Consider it leased," Blythe said, exchanging a look
with Cait that said she was thinking the same thing. She
took out her checkbook and a gold filigree pen, then wrote
a check which she handed to Jill. "I assume this will cover
the deposit?"

"And the first and last month's rent," Jill agreed. She
smiled, obviously pleased to have that little matter taken
care of. "We're having a resident's earthquake survival
party tonight," she informed Cait. "I hope you and Lily
can come."

Cait turned toward Connor, who, satisfied that things
had turned out the way he wanted, had gone back to
hanging the bookshelves. "Are you going to be there?"

He glanced back over his shoulder. "Since I'm a resident now, yeah, I suppose I'll show up," he said with
studied casualness. Actually, he had no intention of missing it. Not if Lily was going to come.

Terrific. "We'll be there," Cait assured Jill. "With bells
on."

6

FLYNN'S SERVED as a community watering hole, a place to sit and talk and share what had happened that day with neighbors. Named in honor of Errol Flynn and established as a tribute to all the swinging bachelors who'd supposedly lived in Bachelor Arms—many of whom were depicted in the black-and-white photographs hanging on the walls—its decor tended to brass railings, dark wood and the black-and-white art deco style tile so in vogue during Hollywood's glamour days.

The three friends claimed the single empty booth along the wall. Ten minutes after their drinks and a huge platter of nachos had been served, Lily and Cait were still arguing.

"I'm sorry," Lily repeated for the umpteenth time, "but I can't stay in that building."

Blythe, who'd been sipping on a glass of iced tea, had remained silent, watching the pair go back and forth, as they had so many times during their college days.

"Can't?" Cait challenged. "Or won't?" When Lily didn't answer, she exhaled a frustrated sigh that ruffled her fiery bangs. "I can't believe you're willing to give up a super apartment, at a bargain price, just because some guy who just happens to have turned out to be the building's fill-in handyman asked you out to dinner."

When put that way, her objections sounded ridiculous. Knowing that her reasons were valid, albeit inexplicable,

Lily lifted her chin a fraction. "It's more complicated than that."

"It doesn't necessarily have to be," Blythe suggested mildly, entering the conversation for the first time.

"What does that mean?" Lily challenged in a way that had Blythe and Cait exchanging surreptitious, satisfied glances. When she'd first arrived in Los Angeles, Lily had been depressed and lost. It was good to see her regain a bit of her old spunk.

Blythe decided that if Mac Sullivan had anything to do with Lily's renewed spirit, she was more than a little grateful for his appearance.

"Jill already said he was only filling in for Mr. Amberson," Blythe reminded Lily. "As soon as Amberson returns home, your white knight won't have a job any longer."

"He's not *my* white knight." The emotional turmoil stirred up by Mac Sullivan's unexpected reappearance in her life had her baby kicking up a storm.

"Point taken," Blythe agreed easily. "But the fact remains that he'll probably be on his way back to the Bay area any day."

"One can only hope," Lily muttered.

She already knew what it was like to live with the pain that came with falling in love. It started out, deep in the bone, and spread and throbbed until it consumed every ounce of your mind, your body. Your soul.

Although what she felt for Mac Sullivan was a long, long way from love, Lily had no doubt that it could hurt just the same. Even worse, having already suffered so deeply, she suspected she was even more vulnerable than she'd been when she allowed herself to be swept off her feet by James Carter Van Cortlandt.

"Blythe's right," Cait said. "The man will undoubtedly be gone before you know it." Having seen the gleam in Mac Sullivan's eyes as he'd looked at Lily, Cait didn't believe it for a moment.

"Talk about the devil," Blythe murmured, glancing over Cait's shoulder toward the door.

Cait's head swung around and she grinned. Lily, on the other hand, pretended sudden interest in the tabletop.

"I hate to bother you ladies," Connor said, stopping beside their table. He'd taken off the tool belt and put on a royal blue polo shirt that did nothing to decrease his sex appeal. On the contrary, with his bare chest no longer a distraction, it was impossible for Lily, who cast a quick surreptitious look upward, not to notice that the muscles in his upper arms looked as hard as rocks. "But I thought I should let you know that the work on the bookcase is all done."

His grin was quick and too endearing for any woman's comfort. Cait thought it was too bad, since Lily was refusing to look at him again, that it was wasted on the two women at the table who'd already agreed to marry other men.

"You can move in any time, Lily," he said, addressing her directly.

She slowly lifted her head.

Her parents had always taught her to repay kindness with kindness. In this case, Lily chose to make an exception. "I still haven't decided if I *am* going to move into Bachelor Arms." Her voice was cool, reminding Connor of the tone an empress might use to dismiss an errant coachman.

Haughtiness didn't suit her, he considered. Lily Van Cortlandt did not belong in a stuffy drawing room; it was much easier to picture her in some mountain meadow emblazoned with wildflowers.

Or better yet, a hayloft. As he imagined her lying on a bed of fragrant yellow hay, her lush ripe body warmed by the buttery rays of a benevolent summer sun streaming in through the open window, a raw, jagged need stirred in his gut.

"It's very nice of you to get the work done so quickly," Cait said.

In his idle fantasy, Connor had been skimming his lips over Lily's body, tasting each bit of fragrant, sunwarmed flesh. Cait's words snapped him back.

"It's my job." Once again his negligent shrug drew Lily's unwilling attention to his wide, strong shoulders.

"Why don't you join us for lunch, Mr. Sullivan?" Cait offered with a feigned innocence that proved her mother was not the only actress in the family. "Since we're going to be neighbors, we may as well get to know one another."

"Cait—" Lily warned.

"Thanks." When Cait scooted over, making room for him in the booth beside her, Connor didn't hesitate to sit down. "But it's Mac. And I insist on getting the check."

Before Cait could suggest that they go Dutch, or Lily could escape yet again, the bartender returned to the table to refill the iced tea glasses.

"Excuse me, Ms. Fielding," he said, "I hate to interrupt, but I was wondering what you knew about the sale of Xanadu Studios."

Cait had introduced Eddie when they'd first arrived. Blythe had found him good-looking in a rugged, outdoorsy sort of way. And while she wasn't at all surprised to learn that he, too, was trying to break into show business, she had been surprised that he was not an actor, but a budding screenwriter.

Now she stared up at him. "What sale?"

Connor bit back a curse and wondered where the leak had come from. The news wasn't supposed to be released to the press until the end of the month.

"You didn't know?" It was Eddie's turn to stare. "I just figured, since you're one of the studio's biggest stars, you would have heard something on the grapevine."

"Actually, I've been a bit preoccupied lately."

Blythe's head was spinning as she considered the ramifications of Eddie's news. She wasn't overly concerned about the projects she'd agreed to star in; as far as she was concerned, she'd love to see the new owner scuttle the films that would cast her in her usual role of femme fatale.

But her Alexandra script was a different story! Walter Stern III had signed the contract; if he was no longer in charge of the studio, did she still have a deal?

"Are you certain about this?" she asked the bartender. After all, this was a town that thrived on gossip. Most of it unfounded.

"It's in today's *Variety*," he assured her. "The cover article says that Stern sold it to some company called C. S. Mackay Enterprises, Inc.... I'll go get the paper." He put the pitcher of iced tea on the table and went around behind the bar.

Unlike many CEOs, Connor kept his public relations people working overtime to keep his personal life out of the press. Now, he was about two seconds away from having his cover blown. Once Lily saw the photo that would undoubtedly accompany the article, she'd know exactly who he was.

"Connor Mackay bought Blythe's studio?" Lily asked, instantly forgetting her concerns regarding Mac Sullivan.

Blythe was about to have horrendous problems of her own.

"Who's Connor Mackay?" Cait asked.

Lily's full wide lips drew into a tight frown that told Connor that whatever Junior had revealed about their business dealings hadn't been the truth.

"He's C. S. Mackay Enterprises, Inc." The way her cornflower-hued eyes had hardened to blue ice assured Connor that if he hadn't lied about his identity, she wouldn't have said two words to him. "He's also greedy, grasping, unscrupulous and dishonest."

Connor managed, just barely, to reign in his temper and keep from challenging her unflattering statement.

"That's a pretty harsh indictment," Blythe murmured, even as her heart sank. Lily had always been blind when it came to others' faults. Which was why, Blythe considered, she'd ended up with Junior.

"Not harsh enough," Lily said. "He's part of the reason I'm broke."

Connor nearly groaned. She was wrong, of course. But that wasn't the point. The point was that about this, at least, she seemed to believe her lying, cheating husband.

"I thought Junior was the reason you're broke," Cait argued.

Amen, Connor agreed silently.

"Connor Mackay cheated Junior in some investment deal they'd gone into together. Junior told me he wiped out our mutual fund account."

Now *that* was a damn lie! Entrapped by his earlier subterfuge, Connor clenched his teeth together until his jaw began to throb.

"No offense, Lily," Blythe pointed out. "But Junior wasn't exactly a pillar of personal integrity. Perhaps he wasn't being quite honest with you."

Lord, Blythe hoped so! To think that Walter, for whatever reason, had turned the studio over to some unethical corporate shark caused a headache to begin throbbing at her temple.

Eddie returned with the paper. "Here it is," he said, handing the paper to Blythe. The headline screamed the sale in bold black type that assured her it was no ill-founded rumor.

"Eschewing a position on the board of his family's vast international conglomerate," Blythe read aloud, "reclusive multimillionaire Connor Mackay graduated eight years ago with an undergraduate degree from USC and an MBA from Stanford business school.

"Armed with his sheepskin and a million-dollar trust inheritance from his wealthy grandmother Victoria Vallejo Sullivan Brady, he proceeded to buy his first company, a little known herb farm hidden away in the mountains near Mt. Shasta."

Despite his current discomfort, Connor recalled the transaction fondly. The reclusive botanist who ran the company out of his geodesic dome house turned out to be a raging hypochondriac who'd greeted him wearing a white isolation suit—like the type worn by nuclear power plant workers, or environmental scientists assigned to clean up toxic waste—and insisted that the visiting businessman scrub down with Phisohex and change into a pair of organically grown cotton slacks and shirt before their meeting.

Never one to sweat the small stuff, and deciding it was foolish to allow irritating or idiosyncratic behavior to get in the way of deal making, Connor had readily obliged him.

Warren Pettijohn might be a little weird, Connor thought now. But he definitely knew his herbs. After buying the company, he'd kept the eccentric botanist at the helm, encouraging him to spread his inventive wings.

"Benevolent Earth herbs and Blue Sky teas have acquired a worldwide market," Blythe continued to read. "And after a public offering last fall, the company was listed on the New York Stock Exchange."

"I buy those herbs," Cait said. "The Mediterranean oregano is the secret to my spaghetti sauce."

"And I buy the tea." This from Blythe.

Lily folded her arms across her chest. "I'd rather starve. And drink mud from the Hudson River."

Connor tried to remind himself that he'd always enjoyed a challenge.

"Mackay went on to expand into real estate, horse breeding farms, computer companies and outdoor equipment," Blythe read. "It also says that economists are unable to find a common thread among his purchases."

That was because the number crunchers in the pinstriped suits on Wall Street had never believed him when he'd insisted that his only secret to success, if indeed there *was* a secret, was investing in what interested him personally at the moment—like Xanadu Studios.

"Is there a picture?" Cait asked.

"Of course." Connor prepared himself for the attack he knew was about to come. But when Blythe held the paper up so everyone at the table could see the accompanying news photo, cooling relief flooded over him.

It was an old one, taken shortly after his graduation from USC. He'd grown a beard after not shaving on a thirteen-day river-rafting trip down the Colorado in the Grand Canyon. He'd thought it might make him look older and more experienced.

Unfortunately, the damn thing had been hot as hell in the summer, itched like the devil year-round and when a luscious bond trader from the west coast offices of Goldman Sachs complained it scratched, he'd shaved it off without a hint of remorse.

"He has nice eyes," Cait said.

"They're too close together," Lily decided. "And you can see the larceny in them."

Although she studied the picture with renewed intensity, all Blythe saw was her project going down the drain. She put down the paper. "It doesn't say he's dishonest."

Hope melded with worry in her eyes and her voice, making Connor want to assure her that his only goal was to make Xanadu stronger. Not interfere with her own career goals, whatever they happened to be.

"I wonder what will happen to my script?" Eddie said, his own expression more morose than Blythe's.

"Your script is at Xanadu now?" Cait asked. "I thought it was at Touchstone." And before that, Paramount.

"After changing the concept three times and giving it six different titles, they finally passed. So I figured, why not try Xanadu? Stern had promised me a meeting next week." He dragged a hand through his short, wavy brown hair. "I guess I should call and see if it's still on."

He sighed and looked at Connor as if noticing him for the first time. "Can I get you something?" he asked, trying for enthusiasm, but failing. "A draft?"

"I think I'll stick to iced tea. Since I'm technically on duty." Connor flashed a smile at Lily. "If you need any help moving in, Ms. Van Cortlandt, I've got a pretty strong back."

"I don't have all that much to move."

Her tone was thick with disinterest that Connor hoped was feigned. He took the fact that she was no longer insisting she wasn't moving into Bachelor Arms as a good sign.

As he thanked Eddie for the iced tea and ordered a Reuben sandwich from the bar menu, Connor found himself looking forward to tonight's earthquake survival party.

AFTER ENSURING that Lily's cupboards were stocked with food, Blythe returned to Château Marmont to find Alan waiting for her.

"Poor dear," she murmured as she tilted her head for her fiancé's kiss. You must be absolutely exhausted."

"I caught a few winks in the doctor's lounge. Actually, it reminded me of my intern days. Although I was a lot younger in those days."

"You're certainly not old now, darling," Blythe said loyally. At forty, Alan was fifteen years her elder, but having worked all her life, Blythe was more mature than most of her peers.

"Spoken like a true and loyal wife," he murmured as he nibbled on her earlobe. He ran his hands down her back and fitted her against him. "I'm sorry about your house, darling."

"It's just a house." Blythe realized that the loss was, in the scheme of things, vastly insignificant.

"We can always change our plans and move into mine."

She wasn't about to get into that argument again. "I'll think about it," she hedged.

"That's my girl." His lips plucked at hers. Blythe waited for the stirring of desire and was vaguely worried when it wasn't forthcoming.

"Do you realize," Alan murmured against her mouth, "that if it weren't for that damn earthquake, we'd be in Maui, celebrating our honeymoon right now?"

"I know." She sighed and wrapped her arms around his waist. If she'd been in Hawaii, she never would have kissed Gage.

"I know it's going to take some time to reschedule the ceremony," he allowed. "But I have a surprise for you."

"I love surprises."

Most of them, anyway. The surprise concerning Xanadu had been an unpleasant one. When she'd tried to reach Walter Stern, his secretary had informed her that he left the country on a vacation trip to Milan. Blythe had not found the news encouraging. Lacing their fingers together, he led her into the adjoining bedroom. The wide bed had been turned down, fragrant beeswax candles had been lit and a portable CD player that hadn't been there when she'd checked in sat atop the antique dresser.

He turned a dial on the CD control. Blythe heard the sound of the sea. "Oh, Alan—"

He cut her words off with a deeper, longer kiss. "This is just the beginning," he promised in a voice roughened with desire.

After draping a lei of fragrant, purple plumaria around her neck, he poured drinks from a glass pitcher that had been left on the bedside table into twin glasses garnished with orange slices and cherries.

"Mai Tais," he said, handing Blythe one of the glasses.

A renewed surge of guilt steamrolled over Blythe. All right, so Alan didn't always understand about her need to work. And perhaps he didn't respect the movie business as much as she would have liked. And maybe he didn't exactly make her blood burn. But she had not a single doubt that he loved her.

She took a sip and found the drink to be, as everything else Alan Sturgess did, absolutely perfect.

"How did you manage all this," she asked, "when you've been in surgery all these hours?"

"It's amazing what you can accomplish with a few phone calls." He smiled and looked vastly pleased with himself. "There's more." He handed her a slim white box.

"Oh, Alan," Blythe demurred as she slipped the ribbon off the box, "you shouldn't have . . ." Her voice drifted off as she stared down at the contents of the box. Having expected jewelry, the familiar envelopes came as a distinct surprise.

"I had them rewrite the tickets," he said. "We leave at midnight."

"But Alan—"

He pressed a finger against her lips. "Doctor's orders. You need some time off, Blythe." His hands sloped her stiff shoulders. "I've been trying to warn you that you'll get ill if you insist on keeping up this grueling schedule."

He ran his slender surgeon's hand down her hair. "So, if you won't take care of yourself, darling, it's up to me to take care of you."

"But Lily—"

"Is being well taken care of by Cait."

That much Blythe knew to be true. And nothing could be resolved about Xanadu until Walter returned from Milan.

She thought about Gage, who was already in Florida, tracking down a new lead on Alexandra. And who'd promised, or, more accurately, *threatened*, to resume what had flared so hotly and unexpectedly between them on the dock in Marina del Rey when he returned.

Blythe was not immune to chemistry between a man and a woman. There had been several times when she'd experienced a crush on her leading man while making a film, but having witnessed the destruction of too many Hollywood marriages because people couldn't tell the difference between real life and make-believe, Blythe was too levelheaded to throw away her relationship with Alan Sturgess just because Gage Remington's kisses could make her knees weak.

Reminding herself that she'd made the decision to marry Alan months ago, reassuring herself that it was a right and sensible decision, as she allowed him to lower her to the queen-size bed, Blythe vowed that by the time Gage returned, she'd have her uncharacteristic, impulsive, unruly feelings safely under control.

"I REALLY DON'T feel up to a party," Lily protested that evening.

"It's not really a party," Cait argued. "More of a casual get-together. And what better way to meet your neighbors?"

"Still—"

"You don't have to stay long. Come on, Lily," Cait urged, "if you'd quit fighting the idea you may just discover you'll have a good time. Besides, you're way overdue for a little fun."

"I don't have anything to wear," Lily argued, falling back on the time-honored complaint of women everywhere.

Cait grinned. "Don't worry. As it happens, I have just the thing." She was out the door, headed upstairs to her own apartment before Lily could point out that the odds of anything Cait owned actually fitting were slim to none.

She would have been wrong.

Cait returned with an ivory gauze dress trimmed in lace that looked as if it had been dipped in tea. Although not technically a maternity dress, the flowing lines could easily accommodate a pregnancy. A wheat-hued underslip kept the dress decent.

"It's lovely," Lily admitted.

"Isn't it?" Cait eyed the dress with obvious approval. "I bought it on a wildly romantic whim last week at Saks." She did not add that she'd been thinking of Sloan at the time.

"You haven't even worn it," Lily protested as she noticed the sales tag hanging from the lacy sleeve.

"That makes it even better." Cait pushed the dress into Lily's arms. "Consider it a housewarming gift."

As generous a gesture as it was, Lily wanted to turn it down. But as she fingered the intricate lace, she felt herself succumbing to temptation. It had been so long since she'd been able to afford anything this lovely. Longer still since she'd felt she deserved anything this lovely.

"I think housewarming gifts are supposed to be toasters." The lace truly was exquisite. "Or blenders."

Cait shrugged. "This is Los Angeles. We don't follow any stuffy rules out here."

"I'll just try it on," Lily decided. With luck, it wouldn't fit.

Wrong again. The silky slip fell over her body like a cooling waterfall.

"Oh, I knew it!" Cait said, clearly pleased when Lily called her into the bedroom. "It's you."

Lily ran her hands down the front of the dress and silently agreed. She studied her reflection in the full-length mirror on the back of the door. "The dress is wonderful," she agreed. "But I still look like death warmed over."

"You are too pale," Cait agreed with typical honesty. "But you just need a little help until our California sun kicks in."

She dug around in the duffle bag she'd brought downstairs with the dress, pulled out a black-and-gold compact, and applied a soft rose blush to Lily's cheeks.

"There," she said, standing back to approve her hand-iwork, "that's a lot better."

Lily checked in the mirror again and decided Cait was right.

"And you need a brighter lipstick," Cait decided, get-ting into the impromptu makeover. "Something with pow." She rummaged through the bag again and came up with a gilt tube.

"I could never wear that," Lily protested as she ob-served the bright scarlet shade.

"I suppose it *is* overkill," Cait agreed reluctantly, paus-ing to touch up her own vermilion lips. She began rum-maging again. "Aha! Perfect. Peppermint pink."

The color, which reminded Lily of bubble gum, turned an attractive rose hue on application. "Much, much bet-ter," Cait decided.

Lily had to agree. She was, she realized amazingly, al-most pretty.

She was the loveliest woman at the party. Connor, who considered himself an expert on such things, observed Lily's arrival and felt his stomach tighten.

Not that Bachelor Arms was suffering from a surfeit of attractive women. At any other time, despite what Con-nor guessed to be a ten-year difference in their ages, he would have found Jill Foyle's blend of sex and class decid-edly appealing. And of course Brenda Muir and her best friend, Bobbie-Sue O'Hara, were gorgeous enough to be cast in any daytime soap opera.

As for Cait Carrigan, her stunning, dramatic looks were designed to bring a man to his knees.

Despite the obvious appeal of the other female tenants, in Connor's eyes, they couldn't compete with Lily Van Cortlandt's fragile blond looks. He watched her for a while, talking with some dapper guy in Armani slacks and

Ralph Lauren polo shirt, who was gazing at her the way a chocoholic stares at a Hershey bar. Obviously Connor was not the only male who found blond madonna types appealing.

Determined to stake his claim now, before the resident Lothario got any ideas, Connor went over to the bar that Jill, with Eddie's help, had set up at the far end of the central courtyard. Then, with a beer in one hand and a glass of mineral water in the other, he headed toward her.

Lily sensed him coming before she saw him. It was, oddly, as if she'd developed some type of radar that told her whenever Mac was in the vicinity. Resisting an urge to smooth out any wrinkles in the gauze dress, or finger comb her hair, she pasted an interested look on her face and continued to smile up at the man who, amazingly, given the advanced state of her pregnancy, had hit on her within seconds of her arrival at the party.

"Good evening, Mrs. Van Cortlandt." Connor's tone was absolutely proper, belying the gleam in his midnight dark eyes.

His use of her married name drew the response he'd been hoping for. "It's Lily," she corrected mildly. Only a man who was listening very carefully, as Connor was, could have detected the faint edge to her tone.

"Lily," he agreed.

His gaze slowly swept over her, from the top of her blond head down to her feet, clad in the gold mesh sandals Cait had insisted made the outfit. "You're looking particularly lovely tonight."

"Thank you." His eyes were overbrimming with a warm masculine approval that jangled her nerves. Uneasy, but loath to show it, Lily accepted the glass he held out to her. "Although I think anything would be an improvement over how I looked the first time we met."

Obviously put out, Lily's companion cleared his throat, drawing her attention back to him.

"I'm sorry," she said, "I've forgotten my manners. Mac Sullivan, Theodore Smith. Mac is doing some repairs on the building."

"Jill told me she'd hired a handyman." Theodore Smith ran a finger over a carefully trimmed mustache. "It's such a delightfully archaic profession. I had no idea you people still existed."

Connor, who could recognize an insult when he heard one, merely smiled. It was obvious that Smith mistakenly believed that having engaged Lily in conversation so soon after her arrival, he had a prior claim. "There are still a few of us around," he said easily. "And what, exactly, is it *you* do, Mr. Smith?"

The man preened, reminding Connor of a rooster showing off for a barnyard of hens. "I work at Aldus."

"I don't believe I've heard of it." Whatever it was, Connor was tempted to buy it tomorrow just so he could throw Theodore Smith out on his ass.

"It's a men's clothing store," Lily said quickly as she sensed the building tension between the two men.

"One of the better ones in the city," Theodore confirmed. "I sold a suit to Tom Cruise just last week and of course Aaron Spelling wouldn't buy his shirts anywhere else."

"I could always use some new shirts. Perhaps I'll check your store out."

Theodore's arched glance raked over Connor's comfortable, faded chambray shirt and worn jeans. "We're quite expensive."

"You don't have layaway?"

When the salesman literally stiffened like a rod of steel, Lily decided that this ridiculous display of male posturing had gone on long enough.

"I'm sorry, Theodore—"

"Teddy," he reminded her with a smooth, practiced smile.

Lily flashed a warm, apologetic smile of her own. "Teddy," she agreed charmingly. "And as much as I'd love to continue our discussion regarding how the 70s retro look in fashion is being translated into decorating, I really must talk to Mac about a leak in my bathroom faucet." Grabbing hold of Connor's arm, she dragged him across the courtyard to a quiet, out-of-the-way spot beneath a leafy green tree.

"This has got to stop!" she insisted.

"What?" Frustration had etched a line between her pale brows. Connor reached out and smoothed it away.

Her fingers tightened on the plastic glass as the innocent touch caused an unwanted prickling beneath her skin. "You know very well what I'm talking about," she shot back at him. "I'm talking about the way you keep looking at me."

Heaven help her, his hand had moved to her hair. Ignoring her anger, he was sifting it idly through his fingers like grains of sand. "The way you keep touching me."

The flare of temper in her tone and in her eyes only increased her appeal. "I like touching you," Connor said simply. Honestly. He'd never been a man to apologize for his little indulgences. "I think I'll do a lot more of it."

They were close now. Close enough that she had to tilt her head back to meet his dark, laughing eyes. Close enough that she could feel his heat.

   She watched, transfixed as he lowered his head, his intention clear. He was going to kiss her. And although Lily knew that she should move away—now!—she could only stand there, her heart pounding too fast and too hard, and wait for the inevitable.

7

HIS MOUTH WAS SO CLOSE Lily could all but taste it. Slowly, as if in a dream, she lifted her hand, raised it to his chest, but did not push him away.

"There you are!" The familiar voice, coming from behind her, shattered the suspended spell. With every atom of her body still on red alert, Lily blinked, turned and struggled to focus her mind on her friend.

"Oh, hell," Cait said, belatedly realizing what she'd interrupted. "Talk about your bad timing. I'm sorry."

Lily had never known that it was possible to feel relief and regret at the same time. "Actually, your timing's perfect," she said, turning her back on Connor.

Cait observed Lily's heightened color, knew it had nothing to do with the blush she'd applied earlier and decided that things were definitely getting interesting around Bachelor Arms. Having recently fallen in love herself, she wanted everyone she cared about to share the blissful experience. Cait shot a regretful look Connor's way, receiving a resigned shrug in return that assured her he was not a man to allow himself to be distracted. There'd be another time, Cait guessed. And soon.

"I just wanted to tell you that my beeper just went off," she explained. "I've got to go to work."

"I thought detectives worked regular hours." Lily knew that Cait had recently received the promotion after apprehending an escaped serial rapist. Along with the boost

in rank, the bust had earned her a coveted place on the
L.A. Police Sex Crimes Unit.

"Mostly we do," Cait agreed. "But a sixteen-year-old
high school cheerleader was taken up to Griffith Park and
raped by a bunch of fraternity guys from USC. Needless
to say, she's pretty shaken up. The examining physician
thought it would be better if a woman detective inter-
viewed her."

"That's horrible!" Lily knew such things happened. But
like most people, she mostly thought of crime in the ab-
stract. And although she honestly admired Cait's career
choice, she couldn't imagine dealing with such depressing
issues on a daily basis.

"True. Unfortunately, it's not that uncommon." Cait's
russet brows furrowed in a frown. Having recently come
close to being raped and killed by the lowlife perp she'd
had to shoot in the line of duty, she had firsthand knowl-
edge of the terror the girl had experienced.

Reminding herself that she had a job to do, Cait shook
off her momentary depression. "I just wanted to let you
know I was leaving," she said.

"I'll see Lily home," Connor said.

"That's hardly necessary," Lily argued. "Since my
apartment is about sixty feet from here."

"Ah, but you wanted to show me your leaking faucet,"
he reminded her deftly.

"It can wait until morning."

Connor decided that she was awfully cute when she
stuck her chin out that way. She was soft in all the wonderful ways a woman should be soft—including being
round with child—but beneath all that feminine delicacy,
she possessed an underlying toughness that fascinated him
even more.

"Don't you want to stay at the party?" she asked, trying a different tack.

"I'm ready to leave." A devilish light she'd already found too attractive for comfort brightened his dark eyes. "To tell the truth, as nice as everyone around Bachelor Arms seems to be, I keep getting the feeling I've landed on the set of "Melrose Place."

"Besides, a dripping faucet always sounds louder at night. Since you're sleeping for two these days, I don't mind working after hours."

"Really, Mac—"

Cait's beeper sounded again, cutting Lily off in midcomplaint. "I'll leave you two to settle things." She'd been enjoying herself, watching the back and forth volleying as she might a tennis match. "Don't be such a hard-ass," she whispered as she hugged Lily.

To Connor she flashed her inimitable, dazzling smile. "It's nice having a handyman who doesn't punch a clock. I hope you're planning to stay on."

Considering himself lucky to have Cait in his corner, even as he wondered how long it would take her to decide to run a check on him, Connor returned her smile with a dashing grin of his own.

"I wasn't planning to, at first. But I've changed my mind. The rent's right and the scenery—" his gaze skimmed over Lily—"is absolutely stunning."

Satisfied that things would continue to move along nicely without her, Cait headed off to the hospital.

"Nice lady," Connor said as he and Lily watched her walk away.

Lily knew she was in deep, deep trouble when she experienced a prick of something that felt horribly like jealousy. "She's also taken."

He heard the edge, wondered if Lily could possibly be jealous and hoped like hell she was. "So I heard. Sloan Wyndham's a lucky guy. So, when's the big day?"

"I don't know." Lily shrugged. Marriage was not her favorite subject. "Hopefully not too soon. They haven't known each other all that long."

"I take it you're not a fan of short engagements?"

"I just think people should get to know one another. Before they make any kind of lasting commitment."

"So how long, exactly, does that take?"

"Does what take?"

"Getting to know one another."

Lily's eyes narrowed as she sensed the trap. "I suppose it depends on the couple."

"I suppose it does," Connor agreed. "Look at us, for example."

"Us?" She arched a blond brow. "There isn't any *us*."

"Of course there is." He put his arm around her shoulder and began walking toward her apartment. Unwilling to draw attention to them by resisting, Lily had no choice but to go along. "There's been an *us* since I pulled you out of that surf and wondered what would happen, if, having saved your life, I simply kept you. All for myself."

"That's ridiculous!" She pulled away and stared up at him.

"It sounds pretty remarkable," Connor agreed. He ran a thumb down her flushed cheek, following the movement with his eyes. "But that's how I felt.

"Which brings me back to my point. I knew, from nearly that first moment, that I wanted you. Which also proves that arbitrary time lines don't work when you're talking about relationships between men and women."

His thumb felt like feathers against her skin. Soft and inviting. She jerked her head back, away from his weakening touch. "Discounting the fact that your statement about keeping me was blatantly chauvinistic, even if you honestly felt that way, it doesn't count."

Once again he was witness to that steely strength he found fascinating. "Why not?"

"Wanting is easy." Her stomach knotted with fear. And, more frightening yet, longing. "Too easy."

Because the urge to touch her again was nearly irresistible, Connor slipped his hands into his pockets, rocked back on his heels and gave her a slow, considering look.

Refusing to flinch under his intense study, Lily met his gaze and let him look, hoping as she did so that he couldn't tell her heart was hammering.

Reminding himself yet again that he'd always preferred a challenge, Connor decided that some things—some women—were worth whatever time it took to win them.

"Point taken," he said finally.

Lily let out a slow long breath she'd not even been aware of holding.

However, if she'd thought Connor was about to throw in the towel, she would have been wrong. Instead, he linked their hands together, the same easy, affectionate way he had at the beach.

"Now, why don't you show me that leaky faucet?"

Her scent had lingered in the bathroom after her shower. Although the floral perfume distracted him, Connor easily detected the problem with the faucet.

"You need a new washer." He observed the steady drip that had left a yellow ring at the bottom of the basin. "I've got one in my tool box; I'll be right back."

Flashing her another of those self-assured grins that both annoyed and attracted her, he left the apartment. His own apartment, Jill had revealed, was across the courtyard.

In the brief time he was gone, Lily ran a brush through her hair, freshened up her lipstick and spritzed some Anaïs Anaïs cologne at her throat and wrists.

She wasn't really fixing herself up for him, Lily assured herself as she rubbed at a spot of rose lipstick on her front tooth. Not really.

Of course she was. Sighing, she blamed her uncommon feeling on raging hormones. After all, everyone knew expectant mothers were often overly emotional. The havoc Mac was wreaking on her nerve endings was simply a result of her pregnancy.

Connor noticed the primping the minute he returned. Taking it as an encouraging sign, he didn't comment. Instead, he went right to work, replacing the worn washer in minutes.

"I'm impressed." Lily watched him turn the water on and off again. This time there was no annoying drip. She was also surprised. There was no way she would have taken Mac Sullivan to be a real handyman.

"It wasn't difficult." He tossed the ragged washer into a wicker wastebasket.

"I wouldn't have known how to do it." Back home, on the farm, her father had taken care of household repairs. After her marriage, whenever work needed to be done around their white colonial home, Junior had instructed her to call a repairman.

"Actually, it's a snap. Next time, I'll teach you."

Realizing that the days of being able to pay people to do work she should be able to do herself were past, Lily overlooked the fact that his words underlined his remark to Cait that he didn't have plans to leave Bachelor Arms any time soon and decided to take him up on his offer.

"Where did you learn to be so handy?" she asked, curious about this man who seemed determined to infiltrate himself into her life.

"My dad ran a construction company." Connor neglected mentioning that Mackay construction, started by his great-grandfather, was a worldwide commercial enterprise and a Fortune 500 company. "I used to work for him after school. And summers, when I was home from college."

Lily liked the fact that, like her, Mac came from blue-collar roots. "You said owned. Is he retired?"

"He died last summer." An avid outdoorsman, Darren Mackay had been hiking in Patagonia when he'd keeled over from a heart attack. Although Connor missed his father horribly, there was a certain measure of comfort in knowing that he'd died quickly, doing what he loved best.

"I'm sorry." From the pain that briefly shadowed his expressive dark eyes, Lily realized that Mac was still hurting. Which was another thing they had in common.

If she was keeping score.

Which she wasn't.

Not really.

Oh hell. Of course she was.

Hormones, Lily hoped again.

"And your mother?"

Connor's smile was quick and warm, revealing open affection. "Still living in San Francisco. She gardens. And takes cooking lessons, which she tries out on me."

His smile widened to that full-fledged grin Lily was beginning to like far too much for comfort. "Her latest passion is Indian food, which means I've been eating a lot of curry lately. While being grilled on when I'm going to make her a grandmother."

His friendly gaze drifted to her stomach. "I'll bet your parents are counting the days."

Lily felt the familiar pang and realized the loss still hurt. And probably always would. "They both died last summer, too. In a car crash."

"I'm sorry. Any brothers or sisters?"

"No. But Blythe and Cait have always seemed like sisters."

"Cait seems pretty great," he acknowledged. "Blythe, too."

"They're both very special." Even if Cait was determined to play matchmaker. "So, were you representing your family's construction company when we met the other day?"

Connor hated lying. And, although he'd be the first to admit that he possessed a competitive streak a mile wide, he'd be more than willing to forego what was turning out to be a ridiculous bet, if he thought coming clean about his deception would gain a few points with Lily.

The problem was, she'd already professed her dislike of rich men in general and Connor Mackay in particular. That being the case, Connor quickly decided that he had no choice but to go along with the masquerade. For now.

"I wasn't really all that interested in taking over the company," he said.

"Oh." Lily was a little disappointed, then reminded herself that she hadn't exactly rushed back to Iowa to take up farming after her parents' death, either. "So what do you do?"

He shrugged. "A little of this. A little of that." It was the truth, so far as it went.

Frustrated, but loath to reveal too much interest, Lily was trying to come up with another tack when he turned the conversation around. "So, what about you?"

"Me?"

"What do you do?"

"Right now I'm answering the phone for Gage Remington. He's a private detective."

"Sounds exciting."

"That's what I said when he offered me the job. But Gage assures me it's mostly boring routine." She frowned, thinking that there was nothing routine about investigating her in-laws.

Connor watched the emotions move across her face in waves. Worry, anticipation, resolve. "Should you be working," he asked, genuinely concerned for her welfare, "this close to term?"

"There you go again. Behaving as if I'm made of glass."

"On the contrary." His eyes met hers and held. Lily detected a glint of humor in them. Humor and something far more unsettling. "I'm all too aware that you're made of silky, fragrant flesh, Lily." He leaned toward her, slid his hand beneath the lace sleeve of her gauze dress and ran his fingers slowly up her arm.

His tantalizing touch heated her blood. A mist settled over her mind. Which was why, Lily would tell herself later, she didn't protest when he gathered her into his arms.

"You never told me what you were doing here in the first place," she reminded him. Although she let her arms go around him, Lily didn't cling.

"At Bachelor Arms?" He was fascinated by her full ripe mouth.

"No." The way he was looking at her mouth was making her knees weak. "I meant, what you're doing here in Los Angeles."

He slid his hand beneath her hair. It bothered him, lying to her at the same time he was trying to seduce her. "I told you, the other day on the beach, that I was here about a job." Another half truth.

Beguiled by his gently stroking fingers, Lily rested her cheek against his chest. "Did you get it?" The mist surrounding her mind was growing thicker. Warmer.

She felt so good. So right. Connor pressed a kiss against the pale blond crown of her head. "Of course."

Later, Lily would look back and tell herself that his easy arrogance should have set off warning sirens. At the moment, however, she could only wonder how it was that his touch could make her feel comforted and excited all at the same time. "Where?"

"Where what?"

"Where is the job?"

"Oh." How could she keep talking about work at a time like this? He let his lips wander down her neck. "Xanadu Studios." Another half truth.

Momentarily surprised out of her lassitude, Lily looked up at him. "You're kidding!"

"I never kid about my work." That was mostly true.

It was difficult to think when he was looking at her that way. Was it her imagination, or were his eyes suddenly darker?

"Why didn't you say anything when Eddie and Blythe were talking about Xanadu this afternoon at Flynn's?"

Connor forced a shrug and tried to ignore the stab of guilt. "They were talking about how the sale of the studio was going to affect their scripts. Which really isn't any of my business."

Now *that* was a bald-faced lie. The first he'd told her. Unfortunately, Connor feared, hating this tangled web he'd woven for himself, not the last.

"What were you hired to do?"

"A little of this." Trying to distract her, he ran the back of his hand up the side of her face. "A little of that."

"When do you start?"

Although caution told him that he should watch his words carefully, Connor was finding it difficult to think when she felt so soft and warm in his arms. "Start what?"

She reminded him of a kitten. A sweet, very pregnant kitten. As he found himself wondering if it was even safe for them to make love, Connor wished he'd paid more attention to that sex education film Coach Rawlins had shown to his eighth grade health class.

"Work." Did he realize what he was doing to her? Lily wondered. "When's your first day at Xanadu?"

"Next month."

"Next month? But why—"

"It's simple," he answered her question before she could complete it. "I returned to Los Angeles early because I wanted to see you again."

Lily knew she was in deep, deep trouble when she found herself wanting desperately to believe him. "Are you always so impulsive?"

"Always." Finally! The absolute truth. "Speaking of which—"

He lowered his head, surprising her when instead of seizing her mouth, his lips brushed along her jaw.

"Don't." Her faint protest was belied by the way she tilted her head, allowing him access to her neck.

"Don't what?" More than willing to oblige, he skimmed his mouth down skin that was as silky as it was fragrant. "Don't kiss you here?" His lips lingered at the drumming pulse beat in the hollow of her throat, drawing a shimmering sigh. "Or here?" Her chin. "How about here?"

The sizzling touch of his tongue at a heretofore undiscovered sensitive spot just behind her ear made her moan. "I don't want a quick roll in the sheets with you, Mac."

"Believe me, Lily," he murmured as his lips moved on to her temple, "there will be nothing quick about it."

Promise made, he touched his mouth to hers with a feathery lightness that took every last ounce of his self-control. Connor had been thinking about this kiss for hours. For days. Imagining it, dreaming of it, fantasizing about it, until it had nearly driven him over the edge.

A man accustomed to control in all aspects of his life, Connor was not all that wild about what Lily had done to his mind, not to mention his body. However, as a man who also knew the value of serendipity, he was not prepared to complain.

Especially not when she felt so damn good in his arms. So soft. So right.

From the hunger she'd witnessed in his midnight eyes, Lily had been expecting Mac's mouth to be hard and greedy. But instead, the kiss she'd been secretly waiting for all night was as soft as dandelion fuzz, as delicate as drifting snowflakes. Having braced herself for power, she was helpless against such tenderness.

He didn't push, or, as she might have expected, try to impress with clever technique. Instead, his mouth was warm and oh, so very giving.

Sighing softly, she surrendered to the sweet seduction of the kiss. Lifting her arms around his neck, Lily allowed her eyes to slowly drift shut. Her muscles relaxed. She leaned into him, amazed at how deftly he fitted her bulging shape to his hard male body.

Lord, she was even sweeter than he'd imagined. Softer than he'd dreamed. He placed one hand against her lower back, holding her against him while the other wove its way through the wealth of blond hair, gathering it into a knot at the nape of her neck.

His body throbbed painfully. Even as he felt an almost primal urge to savage, even as he was struck with the wild idea to drag her into the bedroom and spend the rest of the night making mad, passionate love to her, Connor managed to keep the pace unbearably slow.

His lips plucked at hers, his teeth nibbled from one corner of her mouth to the other. He nipped at her sensitive lower lip, causing a soft breath to escape. Fitting her closer yet, he soothed the reddened flesh with his tongue and drew a faint moan.

Lily had never known such liquid pleasure. Such torment. Silvery sensations swam through her bloodstream; her bones turned pliant, her head fell back, offering more.

"Open your eyes, Lily." His mouth continued to play tantalizingly over hers. "I want you to look at me when I kiss you."

He watched as, with obvious effort, she lifted her slumberous lids. Desire had turned her cornflower blue eyes to a hue as dark as a midnight sea. For a long, suspended time, they simply looked at each other—Connor gazing warmly down at her, Lily staring up at him.

Lily had never felt like this in her life. With only his lips, he'd managed to make her float. Indeed, her head felt so light and her bones were so pliant that she could no longer swear that her feet were firmly on the floor.

Lily knew she was on the brink of something dangerous. Something that would change her life—which had already suffered more than enough disruptions this year—yet again. The thought, while terrifyingly tempting, was not exactly a happy one.

Connor watched the emotions warring in those remarkable eyes and knew that she wasn't ready. Not yet.

Oh, he knew it wouldn't take all that much to coax her into his bed. But then what?

Having already accepted the fact that Lily Van Cortlandt had infiltrated herself into a private corner of his heart he'd never even known existed, Connor was not all that surprised to discover that he wanted more. Much, much more.

Connor reluctantly eased away. "You really are so incredibly sweet," he murmured.

Her heart was still thrumming too hard and too fast. Her head was spinning. But even with her senses battered, Lily knew it was important to stay calm. It was, after all, just a kiss.

But, dear Lord, what kiss!

"I told you I didn't want this."

His body was throbbing, practically screaming for relief. But Connor managed to find amusement in her remarkably cool tone. She may have been right off the farm when Junior Van Cortlandt had married her, but the lady had more class in her little finger than her husband, and his snobby parents, had in their entire bodies.

"Actually, if I remember correctly, what you said was, you didn't want a quick roll in the sheets." Because he could not be this close to Lily without touching her, he reached out and twined a gilt strand of hair around his finger.

"Don't worry," he said when she pulled away, "I'm not going to rush you into anything, Lily."

Lily found the gentle affection sparkling in his eyes even more threatening than the earlier hunger. "I can't figure out why you're doing this. What you want from me."

If it was simply sex he was seeking, Lily suspected there was a plethora of drop-dead gorgeous women in Los Angeles who'd jump at a chance to go to bed with him. From the smiles Bobbie-Sue, Brenda and even Jill had been tossing his way earlier this evening, Lily knew of three women right here at Bachelor Arms who wouldn't turn Mac away.

"What do I want?" He smiled, a slow, warm smile she sensed was mostly directed inward. *Everything*, he told himself. "I want to undress you, very, very slowly. Then I want you in my bed. All night long."

"Dammit, Mac—"

"I want to touch you," he continued as if he hadn't heard her faint protest. "Taste you. All over." As if to emphasize his words, his gaze swept slowly over her. "I want to watch your eyes as I take you—take both of us—over the edge. Then I want to watch you when I do it all over again."

And the fact that he wanted to do all that, and more, was the very reason why Connor had to give her time to adjust to the idea. To him.

A nagging little voice in the back of his mind told him that while he was on this honesty kick, it might be a good time to tell her the entire truth. About who he really was. And what he was doing in Los Angeles. He studied her obvious confusion, and her distress, and told himself that after all she'd been through these past days, it wouldn't be wise to throw too much at her, too soon.

Even as he made the decision, Connor wondered when he'd become not only a liar, but a coward.

Lily didn't immediately answer his outrageous declaration. She couldn't. Not when the words were tangled up with all the hot emotions clogging her throat. Feeling like some love-struck teenager, hating herself, but unable to do a thing about it, she stared up at him.

The silence surrounded them, as thick and heavy as the earlier desire. It took all her strength to keep her eyes

steady. Never in her life had she been so moved. Or so
confused. Caught up in emotions too tangled to sort out,
too complex to understand, Lily didn't recognize the distant sound of bells.

"Your phone's ringing," Connor pointed out gently.

Dragging her gaze from Mac's, she scooped up the receiver. "Hello?" She hated the way her voice sounded so
frail and fractured. "Oh, hi, Gage." She took a deep
breath. "Nothing's wrong. Really. I'm fine."

She turned her back on Connor.

Realizing that she needed time, and wanting to give
them both some space, Connor picked up his tool box and
quietly let himself out of the apartment.

As she heard him leave, Lily experienced dual feelings
of relief and regret.

8

BLYTHE WAS IN MAUI. Gage paced the floor of his Miami hotel room and told himself that he shouldn't be surprised. After all, if that earthquake hadn't struck, she'd already be on her honeymoon.

He told himself that he had no reason to be angry. Reminded himself that he had no business feeling so possessive. But that didn't stop him from calling.

The phone rang and rang. Gage was just about ready to hang up when Blythe answered. "Hello?"

When he heard her breathless voice, a jolt of something that could only be jealousy shot through him. *You're losing it, pal,* he told himself.

"Did I interrupt something?" he asked gruffly.

She hesitated, as if surprised by the stern, no-nonsense-cop tone he'd pulled out to conceal the fact that the lady was driving him crazy.

"The phone was ringing when I was coming down the hall," she answered. "I had to run to catch it."

He immediately felt like an ass. He was also unreasonably relieved to learn that she hadn't been engaged in passionate pursuits with her fiancé. "I'm sorry to be interrupting your vacation," he lied.

"Oh, it's no interruption." Her tone was warm and friendly. And, although he told himself he was only imagining it, Gage thought she sounded glad to hear from him. "To tell the truth, I've been getting a little bored."

"Already?" What the hell was the matter with Alan Sturgess anyway? Gage knew that if he had this woman all to himself on some tropical island, boredom would not be a problem.

Her laugh was as bright as Hawaiian sunshine. As breezy as tropical winds. "I think I've forgotten how to relax. Alan says I'm a workaholic."

"So where is the doc, anyway?"

"He visited a hospital this morning. This afternoon he's playing golf with some of the doctors he met there."

The man was definitely a fool. Sturgess didn't deserve her, Gage decided. Which didn't mean that he did.

"I was lying by the pool, trying to read," she continued when he didn't respond. "But I couldn't stop thinking about Alexandra and Patrick. And wondering how you were doing in Miami."

"Other than being in danger of overdosing on art deco, I'm okay. But I did track down some old guy in one of those retirement condos who remembers Alexandra's early days in Cuba. Before Stern brought her to Hollywood."

"He knew her then?"

"Intimately, if the guy can be believed. And if my instincts haven't gotten totally out of whack since leaving the force, I think he's telling the truth."

"So what does he say?"

Gage spent the next ten minutes filling her in on the less than pristine details of Alexandra's allegedly checkered past. Including the allegation that she was not, as Xanadu's publicity department had stated at the time, a member of the Russian royal family. Neither, if the eighty-year-old gambler could be trusted, had she merely been modeling swimsuits in that Havana casino prior to her screen debut.

PLAY
HARLEQUIN'S

LUCKY HEARTS

GAME

AND YOU GET

- ★ FREE BOOKS
- ★ A FREE GIFT
- ★ AND MUCH MORE

**TURN THE PAGE AND
DEAL YOURSELF IN**

PLAY "LUCKY HEARTS" AND YOU GET . . .

★ Exciting Harlequin Temptation® novels — FREE
★ Plus a Lovely Simulated Pearl Drop Necklace — FREE

THEN CONTINUE YOUR LUCKY STREAK WITH A SWEETHEART OF A DEAL

1. Play Lucky Hearts as instructed on the opposite page.

2. Send back this card and you'll receive brand-new Harlequin Temptation® novels. These books have a cover price of $3.25 each, but they are yours to keep absolutely free.

3. There's no catch. You're under no obligation to buy anything. We charge nothing — ZERO — for your first shipment. And you don't have to make any minimum number of purchases — not even one!

4. The fact is thousands of readers enjoy receiving books by mail from the Harlequin Reader Service. They like the convenience of home delivery. . .they like getting the best new novels before they're available in stores . . . and they love our discount prices!

5. We hope that after receiving your free books you'll want to remain a subscriber. But the choice is yours — to continue or cancel, anytime at all! So why not take us up on our invitation, with no risk of any kind. You'll be glad you did!

© 1991 HARLEQUIN ENTERPRISES LIMITED.

"Alexandra was a call girl?"

Knowing that Blythe had gotten emotionally involved in Alexandra's story, Gage understood her disappointment. "It seems so. A couple of the guy's old cronies confirmed that Alexandra was one of the most successful girls in the business. Apparently, she only did business with the high rollers."

"It's important to have high standards." Her tone was dry. And disapproving.

"Hey, you have to remember that although the lady wasn't deposed royalty, she was still a refugee, Blythe. She didn't have any money and didn't speak the language, and who knows what her life was like before escaping Russia?

"Factor in that survival without a man's protection was a lot harder for women in those days, and it's probably not so surprising that she did what she felt she had to do. The only thing she could do."

"I suppose you're right." Gage heard her soft, resigned sigh. "But may I ask a question?"

"Shoot."

"Wouldn't you be upset to discover that the woman you loved had sold her body?"

"Probably," Gage answered honestly. "Initially. But if there's one thing that my years at the cop shop taught me, Blythe, it's that nothing is as black and white as it seems in the movies. If I truly loved a woman, I'd try to figure out some way to deal with the problem. Because anything would be better than losing her."

There was a brief silence as Blythe seemed to be considering his words. "That's an extremely admirable attitude," she said finally. "Unfortunately, nothing I've learned about Patrick Reardon has suggested him to be that broad-minded."

"I know how important it is to you that the guy be innocent," Gage said.

"He is."

For some reason, her unwavering conviction made him smile. "Spoken like a lady who's learned to trust her instincts."

He couldn't help it. His voice had deepened as memories of what had happened the last time Blythe had trusted her feelings filled his mind. Here he was in Miami, while she was miles away in Maui. There were oceans between them. Yet Gage had no trouble at all conjuring up her complex, sensual scent. Just as he could remember, all too well, the sweet, honied taste of her lips.

"Gage..." Her voice, which had become stronger when defending Reardon, had turned shaky again.

They would deal with the chemistry that had flared between them, Gage vowed yet again. But a long-distance phone call was not the place to do it.

"I'm checking out one more thing tomorrow," he said in a professional tone. "Then, after a little side trip to Manhattan for Lily, I'm returning to L.A. I'll keep you up to date."

"Thank you."

He was not all that surprised when she managed a businesslike tone herself. She was, after all, a superb actress.

"In the meantime, try to relax and enjoy yourself." But not too much.

"I'll try," she murmured so softly Gage had to strain to hear. "Goodbye, Gage."

"Goodbye, Blythe."

There was another long moment of extended silence, as if each was reluctant to be the first to break the long-distance connection. Then, finally, they hung up together.

In Miami, Gage resumed pacing.

Across the miles, on the sun-drenched island of Maui, Blythe stared unseeingly out at the glistening, unbelievably blue waters of the Pacific Ocean and wondered if it was the news about Alexandra that had her suddenly so depressed.

Or if it could be something else. Something she didn't dare consider.

At the UCLA Medical Center Hospital, Detective Caitlin Carrigan questioned the young rape victim, gently drawing out painful details that would help in the rapist's apprehension. Unsurprisingly, the vivid descriptions brought back her own near rape.

Cait would never forget the terror she'd experienced that evening. But what would remain most vivid in her mind was the tender way Sloan had assured her that nothing could ever lessen his love for her.

Across town, Sloan labored over his screenplay. He was working on the scene where Alexandra and Patrick eloped to Arizona, wondering, as he did so, how two people who were so much in love could come to such tragic ends.

Of course his own parents hadn't done much better, Sloan considered. His mother had been a blue-blooded Philadelphian, his father a counterculture war protester, and escaped bank robber. Now his father was dead, killed in a shoot-out with the FBI, and his mother was in an expensive institution in Malibu, her mind—and her spirit—hopelessly fractured.

Cait's parents' track record was also nothing to brag about. Multimarried, they changed partners with a frequency that was remarkable even by Hollywood standards.

He and Cait would do better, Sloan vowed. Turning off the computer, he decided to drive over to Bachelor Arms so he could be waiting for her when she returned home from the hospital.

At Bachelor Arms, Connor was finding it difficult to concentrate on the financial figures Walter Stern's assistant had faxed to him. Difficult, hell. How about impossible? He hadn't taken in a single number. Because his mind was filled with images of Lily.

Logically there was no reason for his obsession—as much as he disliked the term, he couldn't deny that it fitted perfectly—with the lady. He'd always enjoyed women. But never had he wanted a woman the way he wanted Lily.

Cursing, he threw down his pen and walked over to the window, staring across the courtyard at her apartment. Her lights were off, suggesting she'd gone to bed. Reminding himself that she needed her sleep, he tamped down the urge to march over there, pull her into his arms and finish what they'd begun.

"Patience," he muttered as he dragged his hand down his face. Returning to his stacks of dry, boring figures, he instructed himself to put her out of his mind.

Connor was still telling himself that hours later.

Of course she couldn't sleep. As she tossed and turned, tangling the sheets and causing the pillow to fall onto the floor, Lily tried to assure herself that it was nothing more than the usual laundry list of problems keeping her awake. After all, she decided as she retrieved the pillow and tried punching it into an acceptable shape, any woman on the verge of becoming a single mother would be right to be concerned about her future. Factor in a threatened custody suit by her former in-laws, a cross-country move, a 6.4 earthquake, and anyone would suffer an attack of insomnia.

Unfortunately, Lily feared that the real reason she was having such trouble sleeping was currently residing across the courtyard.

Trouble. Mac Sullivan was definitely trouble. He probably found it amusing, stirring up the pregnant lady. In fact, he'd undoubtedly already forgotten all about that kiss.

Any lingering embarrassment was her problem, Lily told herself.

Just as the hot, persistent desire that still flowed through her blood was also her problem.

"GOOD MORNING, MAC," Jill greeted Connor the following day.

Her sunshine yellow suit was as bright and perky as her smile. The fitted, flared jacket accented her voluptuous curves and the skirt, tighter and shorter than was customary for business in San Francisco, revealed a dazzling length of firm tanned thigh. She was wearing her hair pinned up today, although the blond strands trailing enticingly around her face diminished the professionalism of the French roll.

"When you're finished there, I have another job for you to do."

"I'm all done." Connor climbed down from the ladder he'd been using to replace a cracked windowpane in apartment 2-C. "You look terrific this morning. Important client meeting?"

"Why, yes." She looked at him with a modicum of surprise that told Connor she wouldn't have expected a handyman to know about high-powered business dealings. "As a matter of fact, I'm having a breakfast meeting with Troy Marshall."

When his expression remained politely blank, she said, "You know, the star from 'One Life, Too Many Lovers'? The sitcom about the newspaper reporter whose dead wife has returned to help him find a replacement wife, but keeps accidently interfering with his love life instead?"

"I'm afraid I haven't seen it." And, if his luck held, he never would.

"Well, despite the outlandish concept, it's really amusing. Of course, Troy makes the show work. He's quite a hunk."

Her eyes sparkled with an obvious feminine interest that explained the fact that not only did Jill remind him of a daffodil this morning, she smelled like a garden in full bloom.

"Well, I wish you luck," he said.

"Thanks." Her smile was quick and warm. "Anyway, the reason I tracked you down is because I spoke with Lily this morning."

"Lily?" Connor tensed. His gaze instinctively swung across the courtyard to Lily's front door. "Is she all right?"

Jill's blue eyes narrowed with renewed curiosity. "She seemed fine. She just wanted to know if there was a vacancy. It seems her boss lost his home in the earthquake and is looking for a new place to live.

"The only vacancy I have is 1-G. It needs painting, but according to Lily, Gage Remington isn't due back in town until the end of the week, anyway. But I thought you should probably get started. So it can air out."

"Sure." Connor grinned obligingly, even as he wondered what the gang back in San Francisco would say if they could see him now. "What color were you thinking of?"

"I think white is best. For a rental," Jill decided. "Let me show it to you."

Her sunshine scent mingled with the fragrance of the bougainvillea as they crossed the courtyard together. Once again Connor thought that, if he'd met Jill last week, he'd probably be inclined to give that sitcom hunk a run for his money. Feeling as he did about Lily, he was able to appreciate the interior decorator's sex appeal on the same level he enjoyed a stunning piece of art. Or a particularly complex jazz riff.

Jill opened the arched door and walked inside the apartment. For some reason, Connor paused briefly, his senses suddenly flooded with uneasy feelings he couldn't discern.

"Mac?" Jill was looking at him curiously over her shoulder.

"Coming." He shrugged off the uncharacteristic sensations and followed her into a living room considerably larger than either his or Lily's.

As spacious as the room was, it was the mirror that garnered Connor's immediate attention. It was huge, at least four feet wide by five feet high. Cast in pewter, its frame was a wonderment of scrolls and flowers.

"Isn't it something?" Jill crossed her arms in front of her saffron jacket and stood looking at the mirror that was currently reflecting both their images.

"I've never seen anything like it," Connor said. "I'm also surprised that something so obviously valuable is included in such reasonable rent."

"That's what I thought, the first time I saw it," Jill allowed. "But Ken—he's the regular super—" she reminded Connor "—told me that there really isn't any choice. Since it won't come off the wall."

"You're kidding." Connor walked over to the mirror and ran his fingers over the frame, which, as impossible as it was, seemed to warm beneath his touch.

"Actually, I'm not." As she watched him take hold of the upper corners and tug, Jill said, "If it wasn't so old, I'd think it must be stuck on the wall with that same super-glue NASA uses to keep tiles on the space shuttle."

She was right, Connor discovered. The mirror wouldn't budge. "This is really weird," he muttered.

"If you think that's weird, wait until you hear the legend."

"Legend?" Drawn to the elaborate design, he absently traced the outline of a pewter rosebud.

"Although I've certainly never seen her, people say that sometimes you can see a woman in it."

"A woman?" He looked back into the mirror, seeing only Jill in her daffodil suit and himself in jeans and a white T-shirt.

"A woman. And it gets even better." Jill's light laugh implied she didn't really believe in such supernatural goings-on. "She comes with a legend."

"Most ghost stories do." Connor reminded himself that this was Hollywood, land of professional storytellers.

"Well, this legend says if you see the woman in the mirror, your greatest wish will be granted. Or your greatest fear realized."

Another laugh, this one not quite as self-assured. As if suddenly nervous, Jill glanced down at her watch. "Well, I really do have to run. The paint and all the supplies are down in the basement."

"I'll find them," Connor agreed absently as he continued to trace the intricate scrolling.

The mirror was obviously handcrafted. He knew several auctioneers who'd undoubtedly fight like pit bulls over such a prize. Even without the legend, the mirror was worth an obvious fortune. Throw in a ghost who grants wishes and the sky was undoubtedly the limit. Providing, of course, you could get it off the wall.

Although he found that aspect of the mirror more than a little puzzling, by the time he'd located the cans of shell white paint and spread the drop cloth over the floor, he'd put the mystery from his mind.

Until he climbed down from the ladder after finishing the far wall and felt some strong, silent pull turning him toward the mirror.

It was then he saw her. Dressed in a long, pale, flowing gown, she stood as still as a doe on the edge of a forest and stared out of the beveled, silver-backed glass at Connor.

"Well, well," he murmured. "Hello."

He wasn't surprised when the fantasy didn't answer, but instead continued to look at him as if she could see all the way to his soul.

"So, have you to come to grant my greatest wish? Or am I about to realize my greatest fear?"

Again, nothing. Telling himself that this was merely another daydream, not unlike the ones he'd been having since meeting Lily, Connor was not unnerved by the gossamer image in the mirror.

"Well, if I can offer a suggestion, there's a lady in 3-G I could use a little help with." He flashed his best and most irresistible smile. "If you get my drift."

She returned his smile with an odd, strangely knowing one of her own. Then she disappeared. Like smoke.

"I wonder if that's a *yes*," Connor mused aloud.

For a brief, fleeting moment he found himself wondering if what he'd just witnessed had really happened.

"You might be a bit unorthodox, Mackay," he told himself. "But you're not crazy." At least not yet.

Assuring himself once again that the lady in the mirror was merely a product of his own wishful thinking, stim-

ulated by a sleepless night spent thinking about Lily,
Connor returned to work.

Lily was not in a good mood when she returned to her
apartment late that afternoon. She was hot and tired and
her feet hurt. She was also damning L.A.'s mass transportation system. Having always considered herself an
intelligent woman, she figured she could live in Los Angeles another twenty years and never figure out the intricacies of the Southern California Rapid Transit District.

Frustrated as she was, she was not at all pleased to find
Connor in her apartment. She really wasn't up to dealing
with him. "What are you doing here?"

"Good afternoon to you, too," he greeted her cheerfully from where he was kneeling on the floor beside her
front door. His gaze skimmed briefly over her.

She was wearing the red-and-white top again, this time
with a red skirt that ended at mid thigh and looked far
from matronly. She'd pulled her hair back in an obvious
attempt to remain cool. However, in contrast to Jill's sexy,
face-framing curls, the pale strands that had escaped Lily's
braid were clinging wetly to her neck.

"You look as if you haven't exactly had the best of days."

"That's undoubtedly the understatement of the millen-
nium." She tossed a folded page from this morning's *L.A.
Times* onto the coffee table and sank down onto the couch.
"I swear, this city's RTD map was drawn up by the Mar-
quis de Sade." She sighed as she kicked off her shoes and
rubbed her swollen feet.

Although San Francisco's officials were always boast-
ing about the city's mass transit system, Connor tried to
think of a single instance when he'd ridden on public
transportation, and with the exception of a few cable car
rides, came up blank.

"You need a drink."

As he disappeared into her kitchen, part of her was irritated at the way he appeared to have taken over her apartment. Another, bigger part, didn't have the energy to move from the couch.

When he returned with a frosty glass of lemonade, Lily almost forgave his trespassing. "That looks wonderful." She took a sip. "It's real!"

She hadn't had real lemonade since her days back home on the farm. Her father had always joked that you didn't have to look at the almanac to know when summer had arrived. All you'd have to do is come in from the fields and find a pitcher of Kate Padgett's ribbon-winning lemonade waiting for you on the porch.

"Of course." He grinned, pleased he'd found some way to please her.

"Amazing." She put her feet up on the coffee table, took another sip of the tart yet sweet drink and knew what heaven tasted like.

"Oh, I'm just full of hidden talents."

Lily had no doubt about that. "So," she said, steeling herself against his not inconsiderable charm, "what did you say you were doing in my apartment?"

"I was putting a dead bolt on your front door. It wasn't all that safe."

That same thought had occurred to her last night when she'd bolted the chain. "Thank you."

"Hey, it's my job."

"So you say." She sipped the lemonade and eyed him thoughtfully over the rim of her glass. "I'm still having problems with that."

That she was perceptive as well as beautiful was not a surprise. Connor had never been the kind of man drawn to gorgeous airheads. Telling himself yet again that she'd just given him the perfect opening to tell the truth, he instead sat down on the edge of the oak coffee table.

When he took her feet into his lap, Lily stiffened. "What are you doing?"

"Displaying yet another of my inimitable talents," he said easily. "You look like a lady who could use a foot massage."

There was something far too intimate about having her feet nestled so familiarly in his lap. But she couldn't deny that the firm pressure of his fingers against her aching arch felt sublime.

"Don't tell me this is part of your job." Exhausted, she leaned her head against the back of the couch.

"I'm a handyman." The clever touch moved on to her toes. Lily felt her eyes grow heavy. "The way I see it, my job around Bachelor Arms, at least until Amberson gets back, is to be handy. And offer tenants whatever personal services they require."

Caution, along with a strong streak of common sense, kept her from touching that provocative line. "This really has to stop." Her voice held scant conviction. "I told you, I don't go out with men."

"Did you hear me asking you out?" He changed to the other foot.

"No." Lily allowed her eyes to drift shut. "If I recall correctly, you just wanted me in your bed."

"I still do." When she attempted to jerk her foot away, he tightened his hold. "I'm not about to lie and tell you that my feelings have changed in that regard, Lily. But I also figure that right now, you need a friend more than a lover."

He relaxed his touch and skimmed his fingers up her ankle. "So, I'm volunteering."

She wanted to trust him. Truly she did. But although Lily's only sexual experience had been with Junior—which had, to her disappointment, proven not nearly worth waiting for—she realized that Mac Sullivan was too virile a man to be content with mere friendship.

"You make it sound so easy," she murmured.

He tilted his head and studied her frowning face. "And you make it sound so difficult."

"I've developed this strange idiosyncrasy recently." Opening her eyes again, she met his friendly gaze with a warning look of her own. "I've discovered I prefer making my own decisions."

"That's always the best way." He glanced at the classified newspaper page she'd tossed down on the table. The entries circled in red, then crossed out in bold black strokes, told their own story. "However, everyone needs a little help from time to time. Did I mention that I'm a dynamite car shopper?"

Damn him, anyway. He'd hit upon the one thing with which she honestly could use some assistance. After a not very auspicious visit with a banker from the neighborhood Citibank branch, she'd spent the entire day trudging from Santa Monica to Downey, and still hadn't been able to find a decent car in her admittedly limited price range.

Deciding that Mac was safe—within limits—she closed her eyes again. "I don't believe it came up."

"You can't keep riding buses. Not in this town." He reached over and picked up the paper, frowning as he noticed which listings she'd selected as possibilities. There was no way he was going to let her risk her life in any of these clunkers. "We'll go shopping tomorrow morning. For something decent."

Expecting an argument, Connor was surprised when she didn't instantly respond. Looking up, he observed her closed eyes and softly parted lips and realized that she'd fallen asleep.

He laid her feet on the couch, picked up the empty glass from where she'd dropped it on the carpet, carried it into the kitchen and put it in the dishwasher. Then he went into the adjoining bedroom and retrieved a pillow from the bed.

Her scent lingered on the flower-sprigged case. As he placed it beneath her blond head, desire curled painfully in his gut. Unable to resist touching her when she was helpless to protest, he trailed his fingers slowly up her cheek.

"Sleep well, sweetheart," he murmured softly. "I'll see you in the morning."

With that, he let himself out, locking the door behind him. Crossing the brick courtyard, he returned to apartment 1-G. The pungent aroma of drying paint hit him the minute he opened the door, almost, but not quite, driving Lily's sweet scent from his mind.

He walked over and stood in front of the mirror. Although he could only see his own reflection, Connor wasn't a man inclined to pass up any opportunity.

"If you really do exist," he said, "and your gig really is granting wishes, I'll tell you mine."

He took a deep breath, dragged his hands through his hair, tamped down the desire that always came with thoughts of her and said, "I want Lily."

Although he'd regrettably been living a lie since arriving in Los Angeles, Connor had never, not once, in all his thirty-one years, uttered a more truthful statement.

9

LILY WAS WAITING when Connor arrived at her apartment the following morning. Her eyes were bright and clear, revealing she'd slept well. Her hair, held back with a braided white headband, had been brushed to a silky sheen.

"I like that outfit."

Her floaty top was softly striped in pastel colors—delicate pink, pale peach and soft sea green. The full, gossamer skirt echoed the shades of the blouse. A pair of white sandals revealed she'd painted her toenails a soft pink hue that brought to mind the inside of a sea shell.

"Thank you."

"You remind me of a dish of sherbet." He was struck with a sudden urge to lick her all over. "Pretty and cool and absolutely delicious."

His lips were curved in a friendly smile that echoed the easy confidence in his eyes. Lily wished he wouldn't look at her that way, wished he didn't make her feel this way.

Mac Sullivan had her thinking of things she had no business thinking. Had her wanting things she had no business wanting.

"We'd better get going." She picked up her purse from the table, along with some pages torn from today's paper. "I've circled the best choices. I thought, if you didn't have any objections, that we'd begin with the '85 Civic in Long Beach, then—"

"No." He plucked the sheaf of papers from her hand and tossed them back onto the table.

"No?" A flare of anger made her eyes hot and dark. "What does that mean?"

"It means," he answered amiably, "not on a bet."

She lifted a blond brow. "Excuse me?"

It took a special woman to pull off such a display of haughtiness while wearing a pastel maternity outfit and her hair pulled back in an Alice in Wonderland style. "There is no way I'm going to allow you to risk your life driving some wreck of a skateboard on these freeways."

"*You're* going to allow?" She glared up at him, a small, pregnant woman with right on her side.

Enjoying her anger, he folded his arms across his chest. "I believe that's what I said."

Never, not even when she discovered Junior was having an affair, had Lily been so tempted to swing at anyone. Struggling to resist temptation, she gripped her purse so tightly her knuckles turned white.

"Well." She tossed her head back in a furious gesture that pleased Connor enormously. He'd suspected all along that Lily was a great deal more passionate than even she believed. This flare of temper only proved his suspicions. "Shall you call the Rolls dealer and tell him we're coming by, or shall I?"

"That may be a bit beyond your budget," he allowed. "Even with an excellent negotiator such as myself brokering the deal. But if we put our heads together, we can probably come up with a compromise."

His easygoing attitude punctured her ire. She felt her anger drifting away, like air from a balloon. "I really can't afford a new car."

"Why don't we wait and see?"

"You don't know my bank account."

"And you still haven't realized the extent of my bargaining talents. Besides," he said, looping an arm around her shoulder and leading her to the door, "new car financing rates are lower, which lets more money go toward the car, instead of interest."

She glanced up at him, clearly surprised. "Is that true?"

"Absolutely." As they walked out of the apartment into the bright California sunshine, Connor was feeling more than a little pleased with himself.

Twenty minutes later, Lily was staring down at a sporty cloud white Neon parked on the showroom floor. "Isn't it darling?"

It crossed Connor's mind that he'd sell his soul to have her look at him with that amount of overt lust. "Darling," he agreed. "And small. How about that one?"

Taking hold of her elbow, he led her over to a gleaming jet black New Yorker. The window sticker proclaimed it to be loaded with every option known to man.

"It's nice. But I'd feel as if I were captaining a battleship." She frowned as she perused the sticker. "Not to mention the little fact that even with your alleged wheeler-dealer expertise, I'd have to rob a bank to pay for it."

As if drawn by a magnet, she drifted back to the Neon.

"I think your wife has made up her mind," the salesman said with a smile that revealed his satisfaction at the idea of closing a sale—even if it wasn't the New Yorker—within an hour of opening.

Connor opened his mouth to explain that Lily wasn't his wife. Then shut it. The idea, as radical as it was, sounded eminently appealing.

"Look, my name's Connor Mackay," he said, hoping Lily wouldn't notice he'd taken the salesman aside. Not that there was much chance of that. She was running her hands over the roof of the car, stroking it in a way that did nothing to ease Connor's building need. "I spoke with your owner this morning."

"Ah, yes." The salesman nodded. "He mentioned your call, Mr. Mackay."

Connor tried assuring himself that arranging to make up the difference between what Lily's car cost and what she could actually afford was not exactly lying.

Hell. Of course it was. But at least his heart was in the right place, he decided, watching Lily's absolute delight with what he thought looked like a cartoon car.

"For the time being, the name's Sullivan," he said.

"Of course, sir." Another nod. "Whatever you wish."

The deferential attitude was more than a little familiar. And, he suspected, it was a great deal different than the one Mac Sullivan would receive were the part-time handyman in the market for a new car.

Connor felt another twinge of guilt for cheating in his quest to live as an average, ordinary man. But as he watched Lily climb into the sky blue bucket seat, he reminded himself that his subterfuge was for a good cause.

"The lady obviously has made her decision." Although he would have preferred her choosing something more substantial—like a Bradley tank—her rapt expression reminded Connor of a little girl looking in the window of a doll store on Christmas Eve. "Let's get the paperwork drawn up."

Lily couldn't remember ever wanting anything more in her life. Not even that fire-engine red ten-speed she'd wanted for her eleventh birthday. After a late season thunderstorm had taken out most of the corn crop, she'd known there was no way her parents could afford that bike.

But that hadn't stopped her from wanting it. Desperate, she'd wished on first stars, included it in her nightly prayers, and had even, overlooking the fact that the Padgetts had always been Methodists, sought outside divine intercession by lighting a candle at Our Lady of Perpetual Help Catholic Church.

At the time, she'd been convinced, with an adolescent's unwavering conviction, that she'd literally die if she didn't get it.

Which, of course, considering the sorry state of the family finances, she hadn't. Her father *had* come up with a perfectly good used three-speed which, painted with Rust-Oleum and oiled, had proven more than adequate. But she'd never forgotten how desperately she hungered for that beautiful red bike.

And as ridiculous as it might seem to any sane, rational person, Lily felt exactly the same way now.

"Mac," she whispered as they were ushered into the financial manager's wood-paneled office, "it's still too much."

Her hand was on his arm. Connor covered it with his own. "Don't worry," he said. "I have a good feeling about this."

It took every ounce of her concentration to answer the questions that appeared on the man's computer screen. Her name, age, date of birth, marital status, social security number, bank account numbers, address, and on and on until she thought she was going to scream.

She wanted to tell him just to get to the bottom line. Was she going to get the car or not? But he continued to drone on, laboriously typing in each answer.

"All right, now." He turned toward them, his smile friendly. Remembering a neighbor's dog, a boxer mix, who'd looked at her in much the same way, just before taking a painful nip out of her arm, Lily wasn't fooled by his affable demeanor. "Do you have a trade-in?"

"No." Lily didn't mention that Junior had totaled the Jag. And the money she'd gotten when she'd sold the Volvo had gone to pay off debts. "I'm afraid not." Her heart sank as low as her spirits.

Connor reached over and squeezed her hand. "You don't need a trade-in," he assured her.

"Of course not," the man said with a hearty goodwill Lily suspected was mostly feigned. "May I ask what kind of down payment you were thinking of?"

She opened her mouth to tell him that she thought she could afford twenty-five hundred—so long as she didn't spend an extra dime beyond food and rent for the next six months—when Connor said, "Five hundred."

"Mac—"

"Five hundred sounds just fine," the manager surprised her by saying. He typed the figure onto the screen while Lily shot Connor a puzzled look.

"And what price were you thinking of paying?" the salesman asked when he turned back toward them.

Connor pretended to think a minute, then wrote a number, which was amazingly close to what she'd planned to pay for the ten-year-old Civic, on a piece of paper, which he handed across the desk.

The man glanced down at the number, then looked up at Connor, then back down to the piece of paper again. Lily did not find his frown an encouraging sign. Neither did she like the way he ran the back of his finger along his silver mustache.

"I'm sorry," he said finally. "I'd love to put Ms. Van Cortlandt into the car right now. But the owner would fire me on the spot if I agreed to this."

She knew it! Lily wished she'd never seen the car. Because then she wouldn't have felt such a cold, bleak loss.

Connor turned toward her, surprising her with a quick wink that suggested he'd been expecting just this outcome. "I see. How low can you go? Without getting canned?"

Without hesitation the financial manager wrote his own number on a second piece of paper, which he handed to Connor. Watching, Lily found the entire scenario ridiculously male. Why didn't they just say the prices out loud?

Connor leaned back in the chair and stretched his long legs out in front of him as he eyed the paper thoughtfully. The numbers were getting closer to what she could afford, but they were still far apart.

Too far, she feared. Glancing out the window that looked onto the showroom floor, she saw another couple eyeing the Neon—her Neon!—and felt a sudden urge to race out there and tell them it was taken.

The waiting was driving her crazy! Why didn't he say anything?

"I believe, when we drove up, I saw a sign in the window referring to a college graduate discount," Connor said finally.

"Why, that's right." The man turned toward Lily. "You're a graduate?"

"I have a B.A. in history," Lily said. "Actually, I've had one year of law school."

"There you go," Connor said, obviously pleased to have thought of the tactic.

The number came down another significant notch. Enough that Lily was madly trying to think of what she had left from her broken marriage that she could sell to come up with the additional funds, when Connor's next words stopped her whirling mind in midspin.

"I don't suppose there's an additional discount for an Ivy League school. Since statistics show the earning potential tends to be higher than that of most state institutions."

The man looked at Lily again.

"Brown," she answered obligingly, deciding not to mention what Gage Remington was paying her. Needless to say, it was not your average Ivy League entry level salary.

"Well, why didn't you say so?" The man rubbed his hands together, then picked up his pen.

"I don't believe it!" Lily said ten minutes later. As remarkable as it seemed, she was now the owner of a brand-new, sporty white Neon.

Connor grinned down at her, enjoying her joy. "I told you I was a pretty good negotiator."

"You were better than good!" They were standing in the parking lot in front of the dealership, waiting for the salesman to deliver the car. She clutched the shiny gold key ring in her hand as if it were a talisman. Her bright and breezy laugh slipped beneath his skin. "You were absolutely magnificent!"

Swept away with the wonder of it all, Lily went up on her toes and flung her arms around Connor's neck. Her eyes were laughing up at him as she pressed her mouth against his.

Connor put his left hand behind her neck and pulled her close. Reminding himself they were in a public place and to keep his right hand out of trouble, he settled it at the small of her back and hoped it would stay there.

The kiss, as impulsive as the one he'd given her, was every bit as sweet. But this time it was brimming over with a buoyant vivacity he suspected—rightly—that Lily hadn't felt for a very long time.

Connor tried to accept it for what it was, a gesture of appreciation. Friendship. But as she dropped back down again, breaking the heated contact of her soft lips against his, Connor found himself feeling far more than friendship.

"What was that for?" Despite the fact that the quick kiss left his blood swimming, Connor's lips curved in response to the brilliant lights shining in her eyes.

"To thank you."

Connor saw the car coming toward them and knew he'd made all the progress he was going to for now. "Beats the hell out of a greeting card." Leaning forward, he brushed his lips against hers, rewarded with her slight intake of breath when his teeth nipped at her lower lip.

"I've got some errands to run," he said, purposefully omitting the salient little fact that they happened to be at Xanadu Studios. He flicked a finger down the delicate slope of her nose. "Enjoy the car."

As he walked over to the rental car he was still driving, Lily felt an almost overwhelming urge to call him back. Then she heard the salesman call her name.

She turned, experiencing another surge of sheer pleasure when she viewed her shiny new car.

As she drove out of the parking lot, a burst of the once characteristic optimism she thought she'd lost forever surged through her.

By the time she turned on Wilshire, headed home toward Bachelor Arms, Lily decided that the Neon was a sign. A sign that her life truly had turned around.

THIS SIMPLY HAD TO STOP!

A week after she'd moved into Bachelor Arms, Lily stood in her doorway, watching Mac stroll back to his own apartment across the courtyard, and swore this was truly the last time she was going to let him talk his way into her apartment.

It had, of course, begun with the car. By letting him accompany her to the dealer's, she'd given him the impression that she would be equally open to spending more personal time with him.

Not that he'd proven pushy. On the contrary, the evening she'd returned home with the car, she'd secretly waited for him to show up at her door. By midnight, she'd given up waiting. By three that morning, she was ready to kill Mac Sullivan for messing up her head when she already had enough problems.

Although she hadn't heard from the Van Cortlandts' attorneys since moving to Los Angeles, she was not naive enough to think that her former in-laws had changed their mind about challenging her right to keep her child.

She had enough to deal with, Lily had told herself during that long and lonely night. The custody battle, the move, her new job, not to mention the little fact that in a few short weeks she was going to be a mother. She couldn't afford any distractions.

Especially when the distraction in question was capable of making her forget all the reasons she'd sworn off men.

Despite all her protests to the contrary, Lily could not deny that when Mac showed up the following morning, with fresh bagels, cream cheese and red ripe strawberries nearly as large as a child's fist, she experienced a flood of something that could only be described as pleasure.

Telling herself it was only the enticing aroma that had all her good intentions crumbling like a sand castle at high tide, she'd let him into her apartment. And, she feared, her heart. "I shouldn't eat that," she'd protested when he pulled out the carton of cream cheese and put it next to the book she'd gotten from the library. Wanting to make herself more useful to Gage, she was trying to learn the intricacies of skip tracing. "I have to watch my weight."

"It's fat free," he assured her.

"Then it will taste like wallpaper paste."

"Trust me, you'll love it. The company's supposedly run by a bunch of refugees from the sixties who live on a commune outside Santa Cruz and support themselves by making dairy products from cows who only eat organically grown dandelions, grass and hay."

She tilted her head and gave him a long look. "You're making that up."

"Scout's honor, it's the absolute truth." Refraining from telling her that she was looking at the major stockholder of Contented Cows, Inc., Connor spread the creamy white mixture atop a raisin-and-cinnamon bagel and held it out to her. "Try it."

Telling herself that she had to stop succumbing to every temptation Mac dangled in front of her, Lily took a tentative bite.

"It's delicious."

"And fat free," he reminded her. "As are the berries." When he held out one particularly succulent looking strawberry, Lily threw up her hands. Both literally and figuratively.

"I give up."

Her capitulation achieved, he'd wasted no time. Somehow, before she knew it, he was dropping by every day. Sometimes twice a day. And on not one of those occasions did he arrive empty-handed.

She really was going to have to do something, Lily mused as she climbed into her bed that night. Soon.

Patience had never been Connor's long suit. And it wasn't now. But having known Lily's former husband, which gave him some understanding of what she'd been through, he was willing to bide his time. For as long as it took.

One afternoon, he dropped by with an order of take-out Chinese. Over lunch, as she'd demonstrated how she was teaching herself to use the computer Gage had delivered to network with data bases all over the country, she'd reminded him of an eager school girl.

Four hours later, when she showed up at his door, all flushed and pretty in a flowing flowered sundress, Connor hoped that the painful wait had finally come to an end.

"I hate to bother you."

"You're never a bother, Lily." Increasingly uncomfortable with the lies he'd already told her, Connor was always grateful for an opportunity to tell the truth. He caught the shining ends of her hair between his thumb and forefinger. "On the contrary, you always brighten my day." Another absolute truth. He was definitely on a roll!

He was leaning negligently against the door frame, wearing the familiar white T-shirt and those ragged cutoff shorts that could make any woman weak just looking at him, and a pair of sneakers a homeless person would toss away.

His friendly smile and the warm affection brightening his dark eyes echoed his words. Mac was a nice man, Lily told herself. A kind man. But that didn't keep her from taking a cautious step backward.

"I hate to ask." She twisted her fingers together. "But I need a favor."

"Anything," Connor said promptly.

The funny thing was, Lily mused, as he gave her another one of those easy smiles that set off flutters inside her, he meant it. Mac Sullivan was too sexy for comfort, too virile for safety. But she'd never met a more generous, honest man.

"I was taking childbirth classes back east, so I decided to continue them out here."

"That's probably a good idea."

"Yes. Well . . ." Her fingernails were digging into her palms, but unnerved and stumbling, Lily didn't notice. "The thing is, Cait was going to go with me—to act as my coach—but she got another one of those emergency calls. I know it's selfish of me, but—"

"You were counting on having a coach."

She gnawed on her lip in a way that made Connor want to soothe the red marks with his tongue. "Yes."

Connor felt the warm glow of pure satisfaction flowing through him. They were definitely making progress. He doubted if even two days ago, Lily would have been willing to come to him for assistance. Especially for something as personal as attending childbirth classes.

"Give me two minutes to change," he said.

She was trying to be strong. And independent. For herself and her baby. But, Lily admitted as they drove to the hospital where the classes were scheduled to be held, it was nice to have some help.

"I'm so sorry," Lily said two hours later.

She glanced over at Mac, the laughter in her eyes at odds with the contrition in her voice. He was leaning back against the seat. His face was an unhealthy shade of gray and his eyes were closed.

"It wasn't your fault," he mumbled.

"I really had no idea this was the day they showed the birthing video."

Intensely colorful images flashed through his mind. When his stomach lurched again, he dragged a hand down his face.

"It wasn't that," he insisted. "I think it was the Kung Pao combination I had for lunch. The shrimp was obviously bad."

"I had it, too," she reminded him. "And I'm feeling fine."

Hearing the faint crack in her voice, Connor turned his head toward her, opened his eyes a slit and glared at her. "You think this is real funny, don't you?"

"Funny?" She struggled to rein in the laughter that was clogging her throat. "Of course not. What kind of woman would find humor in watching a grown man swoon in public?"

"I didn't swoon," Connor ground out. "Or faint. Or pass out, or any other little euphemisms you might be thinking up. I merely became a little light-headed."

"I stand corrected."

She really was enjoying this. As he viewed the sparkle in her eyes and the curve of her lips, Connor decided he'd be willing to toss his fortune cookies every day, if that's what it took to make Lily laugh.

"It was the shrimp."

"Of course."

Unable to hold it in any longer, Lily allowed her laughter to break loose. It filled the interior of the little white Neon like a musical chorus of silver bells and crystal wind chimes.

"I'm sorry." She pressed her lips tightly together. But the giggles broke free. "Really." As she stopped for a red light on Wilshire, she took a deep breath, tried for calm, and failed. Miserably.

Never one to dwell on failure, Connor put the humiliating incident behind him. "You should do that more often."

"Do what?"

"Laugh." He reached out and traced her lips with a fingertip, leaving a trail of heat around the perimeter of her mouth. "You have a lovely laugh, Lily. And when you smile, you have a little dimple. Right here." He pressed his finger against the indentation in her right cheek.

Her mouth was dry. Too dry. Her fingers tightened on the steering wheel. The light turned green. An instant later, a southbound Porsche ran its red light, racing through the intersection.

Lily slammed on her brakes, as did the cars behind her. Tires squealed; horns blared. Grateful for the interruption, Lily turned her attention back to her driving and didn't answer.

GAGE RETURNED to town the following day.

"I have good news and bad news," he told her. "The bad news is that the friend I had consulting on your case in New York couldn't find any skeletons in the Van Cortlandts' illustrious closets.

"They're old money; they don't live the lavish lifestyles that became the standard for newly rich Manhattanites during the eighties. They contribute generously to charity, their roots in Manhattan—"

"Go back to the founding Dutch," Lily muttered. Lord knows she'd heard that one before.

"Apparently." His silvery blue eyes, which Lily found a riveting contrast to his jet hair, filled with compassion. And, she was afraid, pity. "I'm sorry. I'll keep digging, but—"

"That's all right." Her shoulders slumped. "It was a long shot, anyway."

"Don't you want to know the good news?"

"Oh." She'd forgotten about that. "I could use some right now," she admitted.

"They haven't been able to find anything to use against you, either."

She stared at him. "How on earth do you know that?"

He shrugged. "I had a little talk with the guy the Van Cortlandts hired."

"But surely he didn't share confidential things about the case?" Client privacy, she'd learned from her books, was one of the hallmarks of the private detective business.

"In the beginning he was reluctant to fill me in," Gage allowed. "But after some discussion, he saw the light."

He absently rubbed his knuckles, drawing Lily's attention to his left hand. "Gage!" She grabbed hold of his hand and ran her fingers over the bruised flesh. "Tell me you didn't hit him!"

He didn't answer directly. "The guy had a bogus case." His jaw hardened, giving Lily the idea of how he must have looked a great deal of time while patrolling L.A.'s mean streets. "I just helped him remember his priorities."

Lily couldn't believe it. A short time ago, she thought she was all alone in the world. Now it seemed she'd gained two men determined to play the role of her white knight.

"He could have filed charges."

"I suppose that was an outside possibility."

"You could have lost your license."

"Naw." He smiled and she noted, not for the first time since meeting him the day of Blythe's aborted wedding, that it had considerable charm. "Never happen."

But it could have, Lily knew. And although she was honestly appalled that Gage would have resorted to violence on her behalf, not to mention risking his own career, she appreciated having this strong, supportive man in her corner.

"Why?" she asked softly. "You don't even know me."

"Of course I do." He reached out and ruffled her hair with a large hand, the gesture more fraternal than intimate. "We've talked on the phone at least three times a day, and you're one of Blythe's best friends, which counts for a lot in my book." Lily, who was watching him carefully, noted the spark in his eyes when he mentioned Blythe's name.

"And besides, I've always had good instincts for people. There have been a lot of times my life depended on those instincts. The same ones that are telling me that you're a pretty special person, Lily."

"You're pretty special yourself."

Moved beyond measure, Lily wrapped her arms around Gage. As she was engulfed in his large, strong arms, she decided Cait was right about Blythe being happier with this man. Lily hoped one of them would do something about it before Blythe was married. And it was too late.

Insisting he hadn't gotten any positive results, Gage refused payment. Which didn't exactly surprise Lily. However, knowing he would have billed any other client, and wanting to repay him in some fashion, she spent the rest of the day helping him get settled into his apartment.

The odor of the fresh paint had dissipated, the carpet had been cleaned, and from what she could tell, Gage had ended up with the largest apartment in the building. And, of course the mirror, which was the focal point of the living room, was absolutely magnificent.

Not only was Gage unappreciative of the pewter-framed antique, he seemed dissatisfied with the apartment in general.

Not exactly dissatisfied, Lily mused as she returned to her own apartment. *Edgy.* When she'd left, he was pacing the place like a caged tiger.

Deciding that her imagination was definitely working overtime, she shrugged off the strange feeling and put Gage's behavior down to jet lag. Or perhaps he was merely comparing the apartment unfavorably to his boat. After all, Blythe had said that the sloop had been absolutely lovely.

She'd just reached her door when Mac approached from the nearby stairway.

"Hi, there."

His wonderful deep voice sent her nerves thrumming. "Hi." She felt the blush rise in her cheeks and knew she was helpless to stop the pleasure from shining in her eyes.

"I came by earlier, but you weren't home."

"Gage is back in town. I was helping him move in."

"So Jill said."

Lily experienced a flare of irritation. It seemed Jill made it a point to know everything that went on around Bachelor Arms. And she certainly wasn't disinclined to offer advice—from decorating hints to dating tips. It also hadn't escaped Lily's notice that the sexy decorator spent an inordinate amount of time with the building's fill-in handyman.

"Jill certainly seems to find a lot for you to do."

Her tone was sharper than usual. There was a flinty look in her eyes Connor had never seen before. Was it possible the lady was jealous? He found he rather liked that idea. A jealous woman was not an indifferent one.

"It's an old building. Things go wrong."

"I suppose so." Disinterested in speculating about Mac's relationship with Jill, Lily turned away and began unlocking her door.

"But, luckily, unless there's another major aftershock, I've got things pretty much caught up."

"How nice for you." Connor followed her into the apartment, causing her to turn and say, "Did you want something?"

Although he didn't comment on it, Connor was definitely pleased with her pique. "I figured, since I've got some free time, you might want to work on your breathing exercises. We've got a class tomorrow night," he reminded her unnecessarily. "And we haven't really practiced."

There was a reason for that. The truth was, the idea of Mac massaging her back was more than Lily could handle. "I can do it myself."

"We're supposed to be a team."

"Cait and I are the team," she reminded him. "You were just filling in."

"Cait's at headquarters," Connor countered. "I talked to her on her way out of the building. Besides, the booklet said it's best to stick with the same coach. Whenever possible. Cait's obviously up to her eyebrows in cases right now, and since you and I started out together, we may as well see the thing through."

He had a point. Still . . .

"I promise, no funny stuff."

He raised his fingers in the form of a pledge, drawing a reluctant smile. She was overreacting, Lily decided. So far, despite having revealed his desire to seduce her, Mac had been a perfect gentleman.

"They say practice makes perfect," she allowed, still uneasy about the plan.

"Absolutely." Tamping down the surge of pure satisfaction, Connor closed the apartment door.

10

As LILY HAD FEARED, it was not the least bit easy. Although the exercises were designed to encourage calm, the feel of Mac's strong hands moving across her shoulders, down her spine to the small of her back, then lower still, did nothing to instill calm. By the time they concluded the prescribed exercises, she was as wired up as a cat on hot pavement and Connor, turning down her offer of iced tea, returned to his own apartment where he stood for a long and frustrating time beneath the now familiar cold shower, willing the icy water to wash away his hunger.

Although performed under far more public conditions, repeating the relaxation techniques in the classroom the following night proved just as frustrating. Indeed, by the time the sun had risen the morning after her second class, Lily made the decision to tell Mac that she really did need to get a new partner.

Tonight, she vowed. After dinner.

But then, just when she least expected it, Lily experienced another legal maneuvering from New York. The Van Cortlandts' attorney had subpoenaed her medical records on the pretence that her former in-laws were concerned about the health and welfare of their unborn grandchild.

This blow proved to be her undoing. Dropping the letter, she went into the bedroom, curled beneath the sheets without bothering to take off her clothes and cried herself to sleep.

Concerned when she didn't answer the door, Connor let himself in with his passkey. The first thing he saw was the letter, lying on the rug in the living room.

As he read it, an icy rage flowed over him, more deadly than any emotion he'd ever experienced. He swore in a low, pungent stream. When he'd first met Junior during their youthful years at boarding school, the scion of the old New York family had a bad habit of picking on people who were younger, smaller or incapable, for whatever reason, of defending themselves.

Obviously, Connor thought now, as he crumpled the paper up in a white-knuckled fist, J. Carter Van Cortlandt had learned his behavior from his parents. Bullies, it seemed, ran in the family.

He found Lily in the dusk-darkened bedroom, curled up in a ball of misery. She looked small and defenseless beneath the flowered sheets. Her delicate face was as pale as marble; dried tears had left salty tracks down her cheeks.

The mattress sighed as he sat down beside her. Lily stirred, but did not awaken.

Two minutes . . . five . . . ten. Connor sat there, watching her sleep for a long, silent time. He'd known that he'd never felt about any woman the way he felt about Lily. Known that he never would. But not until now, as he viewed her looking so vulnerable and considered the battle she'd been waging—a delicate, brave David against a ruthless, larger-than-life Goliath—did Connor realize how deeply he loved her.

Her hair was spread out onto the pillowcase. He stroked it, kissed it, inhaled its familiar fragrance. Her lips were unpainted and parted. Unable to resist, he kissed them, too.

Lily stirred. Connor realized he'd wanted her to. Her eyes fluttered open. "Mac?"

Her weeping had left those gentle eyes red-rimmed and shadowed. But the uncensored emotion he viewed in their depths was the most beautiful thing Connor had ever seen.

He also wished that he could hear those sweet delicate lips say his real name. *Here's your chance*, a nagging little voice pointed out. *Tell her now.*

Deciding she'd had enough upsets for one day, Connor said, "It's me."

"I'm glad you're here." Her smile was as soft and delicate as her voice. She reached out, took hold of his hand and lifted it to her cheek. "Don't go."

Fighting off waves of emotion, he said, "Not on a bet." He lowered his mouth to hers.

The kiss was sweet and laced with tenderness. Lily sighed and allowed herself to sink into the warmth of it.

Clawing for self-control, Connor ended the kiss far too soon for either of them. He brushed a fingertip along the blue shadow beneath her eye. "How long has it been going on?"

Lily sighed, considered pretending she didn't know what Mac was talking about, then decided to tell him the truth.

"The day I learned I was pregnant, my husband told me he was leaving me for another woman. Two days later, he and his mistress died in a car accident. My in-laws learned I was pregnant when I threw up at the funeral. A week after that, a lawyer showed up at my house—which I'd just found out was in foreclosure—with a check for one hundred thousand dollars."

As angry as he'd been when he'd found the letter, Connor discovered that was nothing compared to the rage flowing through him at this moment. He took a deep breath and struggled to get a handle on a temper he'd never known he possessed.

"They tried to buy your child?"

She briefly closed her eyes at the painful memory. "At first I thought it was a mistake. An emotional gesture that came from the pain of having lost their only son."

Connor's jaw clenched. "You don't have to defend them, Lily. What they did was reprehensible."

She sighed again as she stared off into some distance. Realizing she was reliving old memories, none of them very pleasant, Connor felt frustratingly cut off from her.

"You have to understand the Van Cortlandts." She let out a long breath. "They've always had more money than they knew what to do with. I doubt if there's ever been anything they ever wanted they couldn't buy."

"Until now."

She nodded. "Until now." Her palms pressed against her stomach in an unconscious gesture of maternal protection. "I tore the check up, told the lawyer to leave and hoped that would be the end of it."

A tear escaped. Before he could brush it away, Lily had taken a swipe at it with the back of her hand, then squeezed her eyes tight.

"Of course it wasn't." The fear she'd been living with all these months gripped her by her throat. "They want my baby, Mac." Her eyes, her voice, were forlorn.

Connor's anger burned hotter. Brighter. With effort, he managed to keep his thoughts collected, his voice calm. "And you've been trying to deal with all this all by yourself?"

Lily lifted her chin when she thought she detected a note of censure in his rough tone. "In the beginning I didn't have anyone," she said simply. "Since I've come to L.A., Blythe and Cait have given me wonderful support. And Gage..."

Her voice cracked, but instead of the sobs Connor expected, a surprising giggle broke free. "He actually punched the Van Cortlandts' detective in the nose."

Connor made a note to thank the former cop. "That's a start." The mood lightened ever so slightly by her breathless admission, he ran his palm down her hair. "Although I think I'd get a helluva lot more pleasure punching out the Van Cortlandts."

Lily saw the truth in his eyes and felt a wave of emotion so strong and sweet that she knew it could only be one thing. She lifted her palm to his cheek. "I love you, Mac Sullivan."

Later, when everything had fallen apart, he would tell himself that this was when he'd made his fatal mistake. If he'd confessed when Lily first admitted her feelings, she probably would have forgiven his charade.

Her other hand was still pressed against her stomach. Taking time to choose his words carefully, Connor covered it with his own.

And then it happened. The child she was carrying turned, moving against their joined hands, distracting him. Making him forget what he must do.

"That's incredible." Entranced, he spread his fingers, rewarded by a series of somersaults.

Lily smiled through misty eyes. "Isn't it?" Only moments earlier she'd been on the verge of tears. Now she still felt like weeping. But from joy, rather than sorrow. "The first time I felt it, I understood what miracles were all about."

She glanced down at his dark hand and thought that the contrast between strength and tenderness had made her fall in love with Mac in the first place.

"I still think that," she murmured. "Every time."

"I can see why." He wondered what it felt like from inside, but before he could ask, he was treated to another series of rolls that reminded him of a diver hurling off a towering platform. "Hey, a perfect 6.0. The kid's definitely got Olympic Gold in his future."

She laughed, as she was supposed to. The tension she'd been feeling eased. Her sorrow faded. Despite all her problems, she was feeling remarkably carefree.

Then their eyes met and she felt something else all together.

"There's something I need to tell you," Connor said. It was time. *Past* time.

His expression was so grave. So sober. Whatever it was, Lily didn't want to hear it. Not if he was going to tell her that he couldn't love her back.

"Not now." She framed his handsome face in her hands and brushed her lips lightly against his frowning ones. "I don't want to talk any more." Her warm, avid lips plucked at his, encouraging a response. "I just want to make love with you, Mac."

She drew her head back to meet his gaze again. In those remarkable cornflower blue eyes Connor saw faint seeds of doubt. "That is, if you still want to."

How could she ask? Didn't she realize that was practically all he'd been thinking about since he'd pulled her out of the surf and seriously debated whisking her off to San Francisco with him?

"Oh, baby." He drew her back against him, gathering her close, inhaling the scent of her hair, the fragrance of the silky flesh behind her ear. "Let me show you how much I want to."

Lily sighed her pleasure as he brushed delicate butterfly kisses over her face. A soft, excited laugh slipped from between her parted lips.

"I never knew," she murmured as his mouth glided along her jawline. She'd realized that wanting could be so sweet. Desire so exquisite.

"That makes two of us." She was so unbearably soft. And warm. And special. "I've never wanted a woman like I've wanted you, Lily."

He stroked her without hurry through the thin cotton of her flowered sundress, caressing her full curves, creating waves of glorious warmth. "I've never needed a woman like I need you." He rubbed his lips over hers with more tenderness than he'd known himself to be capable of. Ran his fingers over the crests of her voluptuous breasts with more restraint than he'd known he possessed.

"I've never *loved* a woman like I love you." And that, Connor considered as he savored the taste of her soft moan beneath his mouth, made all the difference.

He undressed her slowly. Tenderly. His fingers slowly unfastened each button from the scooped, scalloped neckline to the lace-trimmed, petticoat hem. Then he slowly folded the rosebud-sprigged cotton back, exposing her to his warm and sensuous gaze.

Amazing. He hadn't even known it was possible for pregnant women to wear bikini panties. As for her breasts, Connor had once dated an actress who'd paid a fortune to plump up to measurements nature had provided Lily. The room had grown dark. When Connor reached out to turn on the bedside lamp, Lily caught hold of his hand.

"It's okay." His lips touched hers, muffling her soft protest. "I want to see you, Lily. All of you."

She shook her head, even as her lips clung to his. "I'm fat." It was a whisper, muffled by his mouth, but Connor had no trouble hearing it in the hushed stillness of the bedroom.

"Not fat." His fingers dispatched the clasp of her white bra with a clever touch. He scattered a trail of kisses across the slope of her full and aching breasts. "Beautiful."

Wanting this to be perfect for her, Connor was willing to forego the lamp. But he refused to make love to Lily for the first time in the dark.

Without ceasing his caresses, he reached out with his left hand and snagged the book of matches from a local restaurant lying beside a fat beeswax candle on the bedside table. He bent one of the cardboard matches, struck it against the flinty strip and lit the candle, bathing her in a warm yellow glow.

Her heavy breasts were the color of porcelain, but so much, much warmer. Her flesh was drawn tight against her belly, outlining the child she'd been fighting so desperately to keep. The child Connor swore she *would* keep.

He bent his head again and kissed a faint white stretch line that represented a physical and emotional sacrifice that Connor found overwhelming.

"Absolutely beautiful," he said huskily.

"You don't have to lie." When his tongue skimmed her navel, Lily arched her back in wordless pleasure.

"I'm not." Not about this. *Never* about this. He ran his tongue over a taut nipple. The hot wet caress drew an incoherent moan.

"There's a very good reason fertility figures are so lush and round." Wallowing in the delight of the soft damp flesh, enjoying each delicate tremor, he treated the other nipple to a torment just as prolonged. "It's because men find pregnancy a real turn-on."

"Is that true?" she asked on a breathless, fractured sound.

"Absolutely." When his hand moved between her thighs, slowly, with infinite care, Connor felt her body go lax with pleasure. "There's something amazingly sexy about a warm, ripe woman." Even as he enjoyed the sense of absolute control, he kept his touch gentle. Unhurried.

"And you, my sweet Lily, are the sexiest pregnant lady on the face of the earth."

The amazing thing, Lily thought, was that he meant it. Unlike Junior, who could not open his mouth without telling a lie, Mac was staunchly truthful. It was the most important of the many reasons she'd fallen in love with him.

Lily's blood swam, rich and warm in her veins as he continued to treat her to a languid pleasure so glorious it made her want to weep. He ran his fingers up her inner thigh, drawing a soft, shimmering sigh. When he caressed the gilt triangle between her legs, she moaned and pressed against his hand in a silent plea.

Aroused by her absolute, unguarded response to him, Connor slipped his fingers into her. "You are so warm," he murmured wonderingly in her ear. "So wet."

Having wanted her from the beginning, he would not apologize for possessing a normal man's needs. It may have been desire that had first attracted him to Lily, but as he forced himself to concentrate on her fragility rather than her strength, what was happening here tonight had everything to do with love.

There was no storm. No flare of fireworks. The earth did not move.

Instead there was flickering candlelight. Sweet, whispered words. Tender, murmured promises. Fingers linked, lips melded, legs entwined as he slipped into her.

And as the fragrant beeswax candle burned low and the pale moon climbed high in the sky, showering its silvery light over Bachelor Arms, Connor and Lily rose with it.

DAZED, CONNOR HELD HER against his chest as he waited for his mind and his body to return to normal.

He could spend the remainder of his life in this bed, he decided as he pressed a kiss against the top of her head. So long as Lily was here with him.

Pleased with that idea, pleased with himself, with her, with them together, Connor drew her closer. Hungry for another kiss, he bent a finger beneath her chin, coaxing her head his way, her soft, succulent mouth toward him. It was then he saw she was crying.

Although he'd never known it to be physically possible, Connor felt his heart actually lurch. Then sink.

"Lily?" Tears were streaming down her cheeks in silent silver ribbons. If he'd injured her, or the baby, he'd never forgive himself. "Sweetheart?" As he brushed at the moisture with his fingertip, he felt inordinately clumsy. "Did I hurt you?"

She opened her mouth to answer, then apparently thought better of it. As Connor watched in horrified dismay, she pressed her love-bruised lips tightly together. A renewed flood of tears burst free.

"That's it." He was out of the bed in a shot, grabbing up the telephone receiver. "I'm calling the doctor."

"No!" Her voice trembled even as the tears continued to fall. With more speed and grace than he would have thought possible, given the advanced state of her pregnancy, she left the bed to stand in front of him. "Really, Mac. I don't need a doctor."

He looked down at her, unconvinced. Fear created a metallic taste in his mouth. "You're crying."

"I know." More tears. Hot and wet, they created a sheen in her wide blue eyes. Although she'd already laid claim to his heart, Lily's soft wobbly smile strummed a hundred—a thousand—chords deep inside Connor. She went up on her toes and lifted a hand to his cheek. "It was so perfect." She framed his frowning face between her palms.

"So beautiful." Emotion clogged her throat. She swallowed. She wanted to tell him, but as their eyes met, there was no need for words.

"I'm sorry," she managed on a voice that cracked. She sniffled. "I hardly ever cry."

He'd make her cry again, Connor knew. There was, unfortunately, no getting around it. He closed his eyes briefly and hoped that when she learned the truth about who—and what—he was, she would scream and throw things, and call him every name in the book, all of which he'd be the first to admit he deserved.

Then, because he could not accept the alternative, Connor imagined, after her understandable display of temper, because she possessed a loving heart and generous nature, she would forgive him.

Lily saw the dark emotion swirling in his eyes and misunderstood it for continued concern. "Tell me again."

The way she was looking up at him, with such uncensored love and absolute trust, gave Connor an idea of how Benedict Arnold must have felt. But Arnold had only betrayed his country. His crime, betraying the woman he loved, was far worse.

"Tell you what?"

"That you love me." The dancing light was back in her eyes, her generous mouth widened into a smile that could steal a man's breath, along with his heart, away.

"I love you." Overwhelmed by another surge of fear, this time of losing her, he dragged her tight against him. "Love you." He rained hot, desperate kisses over her face, her neck, her throat. "There's something I want you to promise me."

Her hands were gripping his shoulders. Her lips were as hot and avid as his. "Anything."

With an arm behind her knees, he scooped her up and carried her the few short feet back to the bed. Feeling some desperate masculine need to claim Lily for his own, for always, he braced himself over her.

"Whatever happens," he demanded, his hot eyes locked to hers, "promise that you'll never forget that I love you."

Puzzlement at his intensity flickered briefly over her face. "Of course I won't."

Before she could give voice to the questions he saw swirling in those remarkable eyes, he covered her mouth with his, and surged into her. This time the flight was hard and fast. Moving with him, Lily clung as they soared like a comet into the mists.

NOT FAR AWAY, in apartment 1-G, Gage paced the floor of his apartment, frustrated by the news he'd just received regarding Natasha Kuryan, Alexandra's former makeup artist at Xanadu. When he'd first informed Blythe that the elderly woman had embarked on a cruise to Greece, she'd been understandably frustrated. Having finally located someone who'd actually known the former actress personally, she'd been anxious for a meeting.

At the time he'd counseled patience. The cruise was only for two weeks, he'd reminded her. By the time Blythe returned from her honeymoon, Natasha would be back from Greece.

Knowing that Blythe was waiting for news of his interview with Natasha, Gage decided that since she was going to have to learn the truth sometime, it may as well be now.

Assuring himself that his only motive was to report this latest twist in the complex case to his client, Gage picked up the phone and dialed the Maui Marriott.

"I don't believe it!" Blythe had taken the phone by the pool, where she was working on her tan while Alan pursued birdies and eagles on the resort's emerald green golf course. She did some rapid calculation. "The woman must be in her eighties!"

"I'd say that's a good guess," Gage agreed.

"You know, I really hate it when you stay so calm when I'm not," Blythe complained.

"Sorry."

She heard the repressed humor in his tone over the long-distance telephone line. "It's not funny!"

"Yes, ma'am."

"Dammit, Gage." His drawled, easygoing tone amused even as it frustrated. Blythe found herself smiling in spite of her pique. "It was bad enough when she took off on that cruise. But now you tell me she's having some wild affair—"

"I don't know how wild it is. But she's definitely jumped ship and moved into Kyriako Papakosta's home on the island of Naxos. He's a popular novelist, practically lionized in the country. Anyway, my contact says they were seen dancing cheek-to-cheek in a village taverna."

"How nice," Blythe said dryly.

Natasha Kuryan may be in her twilight years, but it appeared she had more of a social life than Blythe was currently experiencing. For all Alan's alleged need to "get away," he was spending the majority of his time doing exactly what he did in Los Angeles—playing hospital politics.

"Don't worry, if she's not back in a couple of weeks, we'll track her down."

"We?"

"You were the one who wanted to talk to her. If you want to go to Greece alone—"

"No." Blythe cut him off. "I wouldn't even know how to get to Naxos, let alone find Natasha when I arrived." Across the pool, a couple—honeymooners, the concierge had informed Blythe with a knowing grin the other day— were standing in the shallow end, sharing a kiss.

The prolonged embrace reminded Blythe all too vividly of that stolen kiss she'd shared with Gage. Knowing she was in trouble when the mere memory of his firm lips pressed against hers could make her blood warm, she told herself that to run off to some sun-drenched Mediterranean island with a man who'd been playing the starring role in too many of her dreams lately, was horrendously risky.

"Blythe?" His deep husky voice slid beneath her skin, triggering dangerous emotions. "Are you still there?"

"Yes." The single word came out soft and fractured. Blythe dragged her hand through her hair. "Yes, I'm still here. And yes, I think your idea of going to Greece is a good one."

Dear Lord, she was going to do it. As a significant little silence settled over them, she realized that she was not the only one who realized the significance of that decision.

"Oh, one more thing before I hang up," Gage said. "About Lily."

"Lily?" Any lingering desire instantly disintegrated. Blythe sat bolt upright. "Is anything wrong?"

"Actually, it seems as if, for the first time, something might be going very, very right for the lady. She and Mac Sullivan appear to be an item."

"Really?" So Cait had been right about Mac.

"They've been spending a lot of time together. And Cait tells me he took her place as Lily's birthing coach."

"Gracious." Blythe frowned. While she wanted Lily to be happy, she certainly didn't want her jumping into another unhappy relationship. "That is fast work." *Too fast, perhaps.*

"It may seem that way," Gage allowed. "But sometimes, things just click between a man and a woman."

His voice dropped to its lower registers. Once again he was no longer merely a private investigator reporting to a client, but much, much more. His intimate tone told Blythe he was no longer talking about Lily and Mac.

"Well." Blythe forced a breezy smile into her voice. "I'm sure she's in good hands."

"I'll break the guy's face if he does anything to hurt her," Gage promised. "You know, maybe I should check him out. Just in case."

Wanting to protect Lily from further heartache, Blythe was seriously tempted. But, knowing what it would do to their friendship if Lily found out she'd had Mac investigated, she said, "We'd better not. But I'd appreciate you looking out for her. Since you're living at Bachelor Arms."

"I'll watch her like a big brother."

"Thank you." His promise was enough. Blythe only hoped Lily wouldn't need Gage's expert intervention.

There was another pregnant pause, as if they both were reluctant to hang up, though there was nothing left to say.

"Well, have fun," Gage said finally.

Blythe watched the young couple walking arm in arm to their bungalow. It took not the slightest bit of imagination to determine how they planned to spend the rest of their afternoon.

"Thanks." She tamped down her envy. "I'll see you when I get back."

"I'll be waiting."

There was another brief pause. Then a click. Then he was gone.

Sighing, Blythe pushed the button on the cordless phone, leaned back in the lounge and tried to return her attention to the novel she'd been staring at for the past two days.

Unbidden, her rebellious mind conjured up scenes of her and Gage making mad, passionate love. For some inexplicable reason, instead of the glorious tropical Hawaiian landscape surrounding her, Blythe fantasized them surrounded by jagged mountain peaks and glistening, frosty white snow.

THAT NIGHT, in Los Angeles, Cait wandered idly around Sloan's spacious office. The room, with its spectacular view of the Pacific Ocean took up several hundred square feet of his Pacific Palisades home. As she sipped a glass of wine and gazed out at the moon-gilded black satin waters, she wondered how anyone could get any work done when faced with such a dazzling view.

It definitely said something about Sloan's power of concentration, she decided, remembering how she'd once thought him to be yet another hedonistic Hollywood playboy. As it was, she'd arrived from headquarters nearly an hour ago, and except for a brief, almost husbandly kiss, every iota of his attention had been riveted on that damn computer screen.

"That must be some scene," she offered.

"I think it's going to be good," he agreed without looking up. His fingers didn't cease their tap, tap, tapping on the keys. "Gage unearthed some stuff about Alexandra and Patrick's honeymoon from some old clippings that had been misfiled in the Xanadu archives."

"After they eloped to Arizona." Between Blythe and Sloan, Cait figured she probably knew more about the couple than anyone in Hollywood. Everyone except Natasha Kuryan, she thought, unable to resist smiling at the thought of the senior citizen's still unorthodox love life.

"Yeah. I thought I'd play with the scene a bit while it was still fresh in my mind."

His dark hair had fallen over his forehead in a way that made her fingers literally itch to brush it away. "Good idea."

Tired of being ignored and deciding to test her fiancé's powers of concentration, Cait unbuttoned the navy blue skirt she'd worn to headquarters today. She lowered the zipper, certain that the unmistakable sound would garner Sloan's attention.

Nothing.

Undeterred by his seeming lack of interest, she stepped out of the skirt, leaving it on the rug.

Her fingers moved to the pearl buttons of her ivory silk blouse. "So, where was this honeymoon?"

"Colorado."

"Ah." She unfastened each gleaming button one at a time. Sloan muttered a faint curse and began madly back spacing, erasing a line of dialogue. "I've always liked Colorado." She shrugged her shoulders, allowing the blouse to fall unnoticed to the floor, where it lay in a creamy pool beside the skirt.

"Of course it can get extremely cold." She walked over to the oversize desk and perched on the corner. "But, I suppose, if they were on their honeymoon, that wouldn't be a problem." She crossed her long legs. "Seeing as how Patrick probably managed to keep Alexandra warm."

"I imagine so." The sultry swish of silk on silk, combined with the lush sensuality of her tone, belatedly captured Sloan's attention. He lifted his gaze from the screen. His whiskey brown eyes darkened as they took in her long legs, clad in ivory stockings held up by a lacy garter belt.

"Have I ever mentioned I love your undercover clothes?" Seduced by the lure of Cait's sensual pose, he immediately forgot all about his screenplay.

"I believe it's come up." Anticipation flowed through her as his long fingers began toying with the lacy elastic fastener. "It's much nicer, of course, now that I've made detective. I don't have to wear those ugly white uniform undershirts anymore."

"I liked you in white undershirts." He bent his head, moistening the ivory lace covering her breasts with his tongue. "But, I'll have to admit, I like you in lace and silk even better."

His hands continued their torment of her thighs as he unfastened the front clasp with his teeth. There were advantages, Cait admitted as his mouth fastened on a tingling breast, of falling in love with a man who knew his way around women's lingerie.

"But—" he unfastened one stocking and began rolling it slowly, seductively, down her leg "—I think I like you best when you're not wearing anything at all."

How had the tables turned so quickly? Cait wondered as his stroking touch caused her head to spin and her blood to warm. She'd been the one with seduction on her mind. But, as she linked her arms around his neck and invited him to lower her to the gleaming desk, she pressed her mouth to Sloan's and allowed herself to be thoroughly, gloriously seduced.

GAGE WAS ON his second Scotch when he thought he caught a glimpse of something out of the corner of his eye. Turning around, he found himself staring straight into the elaborate mirror. All he could see was his own reflection glowering back at him.

It was only his imagination, he told himself. He was, as always, after talking with Blythe, edgy. Edgy and hot.

When his mind began conjuring up images of Patrick and Alexandra, engaged in passionate pursuits hotter than the waters of the natural hot spring boiling around them, Gage belatedly remembered that he'd forgotten to tell Blythe about having discovered that the ill-fated newlyweds had spent their honeymoon in the Colorado Rockies.

11

WONDERLAND. Two weeks after having made love to Mac, Lily was still living in Wonderland. She woke every morning in his strong, wonderful arms, went to bed every night the same way. During the day, while Mac was away from Bachelor Arms—at his new job at Xanadu—she managed to keep worries about the Van Cortlandts' next move at bay by immersing herself in her work for Gage, which she found absolutely fascinating.

Having always enjoyed research during her college days, she was never bored by the need to explore the nooks and crannies along paper trails that revealed all the complexities of human relationships. Some of the stories her computerized data bases uncovered had more love and betrayal, comedies and tragedies than a fat summer novel.

On one memorable occasion, she'd been poring through *Coles*, a reverse telephone directory, searching out an address for a missing persons case when a man arrived at the office-apartment.

"Where's Gage?" he demanded without offering any greeting.

She recognized the voice immediately. Harold Ames was the son of one of Gage's former sergeants. An accountant by trade, he was paranoid by nature, calling almost daily with reports of new conspiracies which Gage always defused by ensuring him that he was on the case. During the time she'd worked for the detective, Lily had never typed a bill for this man.

"He's out of the office right now." She offered her most calming, encouraging smile. "I'm Lily. May I help you?"

His eyes, beneath the brim of a blue Dodgers cap, narrowed. "You sound familiar."

She nodded and slipped her fingers beneath the desk to the silent alarm Gage had installed. Just in case. "We've talked on the phone."

Another long look. Then, as if unable to keep this latest threat to himself any longer, he blurted out, "Gage has to protect me."

"From whom?"

"The aliens who are bombarding my brain with their silent radio waves."

"I see." Lily nodded again, revealing not a single bit of skepticism. "Can you tell what they're saying?"

"Of course! They want me to surrender when their ship arrives at the Santa Monica pier tomorrow. At midnight. A war on their planet, Janurous, has left a shortage of men. They need me to impregnate their women so the race won't die out."

"Gracious. That is serious." She eyed him with concern. "Do you want to go with them?"

"Are you kidding?" He shot her a look of blatant disbelief. "Have you ever seen a Janurian female?"

"I'm afraid not."

He shuddered. "You're lucky. I have. The last time they took me hostage." His eyes turned wild. "I don't have any will when they bombard my mind this way. Gage has to do something!"

"You know," Lily said slowly, thoughtfully, "I recently read something about alien mind bombardment."

"You did?" He looked surprised.

"Yes. And it seems that the only thing that can stop the ultrasound waves from penetrating the brain's cortex is aluminum foil."

"Reynolds Wrap?"

"Exactly. The article said that a layer of foil lining a hat effectively bounces the rays back into the ozone, where they safely dissipate."

He seemed to be considering that. "Regular tin foil? Or extrastrength broiler?"

"Broiler," she answered promptly. "They are, after all, very strong rays."

"Tell me about it," he muttered. His expression cleared. As she watched, the beleaguered accountant visibly relaxed. "Thank you."

Her smile was as sincere as it was warm. "I was just doing my job."

With that extraterrestrial crisis temporarily solved, Lily returned to work.

"That was great work," Gage told her the next day after she'd managed to locate a deadbeat dad working as a roofer in Fargo, North Dakota.

"I just did what you told me to do." Last night, while Mac had made his mother's recipe for chicken curry, she'd sat at the kitchen table with a dry eraser board and a blue marker, trying out every possible combination of the father of five's names. Gage had taught her that most people, when they seek a new identity, stick with familiar names.

"True. But putting his father's middle name together with his wife's maiden name was a stroke of genius."

Lily flushed with pride and pleasure. "Thank you."

"It's me who should be thanking you. You've made a real difference, Lily." He paused, eyeing her thoughtfully as he rubbed his chin. "I realize that after the baby's born, you're going to be busy. But have you made any plans for after that?"

"Not really." In the beginning, after Junior's death, Lily had been too busy trying to pay off all the debts and remain financially afloat to think about a future. Then dealing with the treacherous Van Cortlandts took all her mental energy.

These days, content to drift along, basking in Mac's love, she'd been putting off making any decisions regarding her future. "Cait suggested I go back to law school."

"What do you think about that?"

"I don't know." Lily shrugged as she began arranging a stack of motor vehicle reports. "Law school is terribly demanding. Even if I could swing it financially, I'd have to leave my baby in day care more hours than I'd like." Deciding it was time for one of them to bring it up, she looked at Gage and said, "Actually, I was hoping I could keep working here for you."

"Actually, I was kind of thinking along those same lines."

His warm smile reached his eyes, reminding her yet again what a very nice man Gage Remington was. She wondered what was going to happen when Blythe returned from Hawaii tomorrow and then reminded herself that her friend's love life was none of her business.

The problem was, having falling in love with Mac had made such a dazzling difference in her life, Lily wanted all her friends to be as happy as she was.

Her mind having momentarily wandered, Lily suddenly realized she'd missed a vital part of the conversation. "Excuse me?"

"I asked if you'd be willing to consider becoming a partner."

"A partner? Like a business partner? With you?"

"That was the idea." He folded his arms across his broad chest, leaned against the edge of the desk and smiled down at her. "But if you've made other plans—"

"No!" She rubbed at her temple, trying to take it all in. "It's just such a surprise. I mean, I thought I was doing a pretty good job, but..." Nonplussed, her voice drifted off as she stared up at him.

"I think we make a good team, Lily. Having you here has freed me up to do outside work. You run the office with all the efficiency of NASA Control, while at the same time making all the clients feel important, even crazy ones like Harold.

"You're already one of the best skip tracers I've ever seen, and unless all my instincts have gone on the blink, I'd say we get along pretty well."

"Better than well," Lily agreed. Gage was, she'd considered on more than one occasion, the big brother she'd always wished she had.

"So, what do you say?"

"What about money?"

"You'd receive an equal percent of the monthly profits," he said. "Which should triple your salary—especially since the way you've made things so efficient has allowed me to take on more cases."

Lily's first thought was the raise would definitely allow her to do some long-overdue shopping for baby clothes and furniture.

Her second thought was that unfortunately, the offer was too generous.

"There's only one problem," she said.

"What problem is that?"

"It wouldn't be fair for me to take half the profits, when I hadn't made half the investment."

"That's not true. The difference you've made—"

"It's not the same," she insisted. "You started this firm with your own money, Gage. Cait told me how you cashed out your savings and took a tax penalty by using your IRA funds just to keep going the first quarter."

"That's true. Did she also tell you that I borrowed a significant amount of money from a Beverly Hills restaurateur who was grateful for me having interrupted a robbery in progress at his upscale pizza place?"

"No, but—"

"The point I'm trying to make," Gage said, effectively overriding her planned protest, "is that we all need a little help from time to time, Lily. If it'd make you feel better, you can put a portion of your salary back into the firm for a few months to even up the investment. Even though it isn't necessary."

She lifted her chin. "It is to me."

"Lord." He raked his hands through his thick black hair. "No wonder you and Cait are friends. You're every bit as stubborn as she is." His smile took the sting out of the frustrated accusation.

"I know." Lily flashed him a smile of her own.

Her eyes turned sober. She had an important decision to make. One that would impact on her and her child. It also crossed her mind that with the jump in salary a partnership would bring, she and Mac would be able to buy a house.

The idea of a small white house in a nice neighborhood, with a fenced back yard big enough for a sandbox and swing set, made her smile. Perhaps, she considered, they could even get a dog. She'd always liked cocker spaniels. And they were supposed to be good with children.

"I'll tell you what," Gage suggested. "Why don't you think about it over the weekend? Talk it over with Mac? We can discuss it some more on Monday."

"Thank you." Lily nodded. "I'd like that." The phone rang. "Remington Investigations," she answered with a brisk yet friendly tone. "Yes, Mr. Potter, Mr. Remington is in his office. I'll transfer you."

As Gage took the call, Lily considered that Remington and Sullivan had a very nice ring.

"It sounds like a great offer," Connor agreed that evening as they took a drive down the California coast. "If you're asking for advice, I'd say, take it."

"I feel guilty about not having any money to put up."

"Gage's plan sounds more than fair. And besides, he's right about you having already made a contribution by freeing him up for more field work."

"True." Although Mac hadn't brought up marriage yet, Lily had to know. She looked over at him. "What do you think about working mothers?"

Connor knew why she was asking, knew he'd been remiss in not having popped the question sooner, but didn't quite know how to explain that she'd be agreeing to be Mrs. Connor Mackay. That was what this weekend trip was about. They needed to be away from Bachelor Arms, away from everyone they knew, so he could finally tell her the truth.

And then, if Lily was still speaking to him—and Connor could not permit himself to think that she might not be—he intended to propose.

"I think," he said slowly, carefully, "that mothers, like everyone else, should try to do what makes them happiest. Because if they're happy, it follows that their children will be happy, too."

It was exactly the answer she'd been hoping for. Lily told herself yet again how very lucky she was to have Mac in her life.

"Where are we going?" All she knew was that when she'd returned to her own apartment, Gage had met her at the door with her suitcase packed and the news that he was taking her away for the weekend.

"It's a surprise."

His lips were curved in their trademark grin, but Lily thought she viewed little seeds of worry in his eyes. Telling herself she was imagining it, she leaned back against the seat and allowed herself to relax.

The sky blue arch sweeping across San Diego Bay was the most graceful bridge Lily had ever seen. She was further entranced by the quaint village environment of Coronado Island itself, with its quiet tree-lined streets of Victorian and Edwardian homes and California bungalows.

"It's absolutely enchanting," she murmured, finding it difficult to believe that the city of San Diego was just a couple of minutes away.

Connor took her hand in his. "I'm glad you like it. I wanted this weekend to be special."

From the huskiness in his voice, Lily suspected that Mac was planning more than a stolen weekend of lovemaking. Perhaps he'd arranged this time away from the others to propose. And, although common sense told her that it was too soon, a deep-seated feminine intuition assured her that she'd never find another man she could love—and who loved her—like Mac Sullivan.

Which was why, sometime between loading the suitcases in the car and crossing the bridge, she'd decided that if Mac did ask her to marry him, she would say yes.

"Mac!" Her eyes widened as he pulled up in front of the magnificent Hotel Del Coronado. "You can't possibly afford this hotel!"

She gazed in wonderment at the red-and-white Victorian structure that stood as a monument to the gilded past. With its intriguing turrets, cupolas and colorful gardens, the hotel belonged on the pages of a storybook.

"Don't worry that pretty head about prices." He leaned across the span between the seats and kissed her. "I've been saving my pennies."

"But—"

He pressed his fingers against her frowning lips. "Just trust me, okay?"

"I do." The truth vibrated in her fervent tone and was echoed in her eyes, making Connor feel like a bastard for having lied to her all these weeks.

He could only hope that she'd still feel the same way about him on Monday morning.

It was a glorious weekend. One Lily knew she'd remember for the rest of her life. They strolled hand in hand along the beach, basked in the sun beside the gleaming Olympic-size swimming pool, took a walking tour of the hotel—where they learned the building had been originally electrified by Thomas Edison—then rented a boat at the Glorietta Bay Marina.

They shared morning pastries in bed and treated themselves to a fabulous dinner in the Prince Edward Grill, where, the waiter informed them, the special gold-trimmed china had been created for the Prince of Wales for that fatal visit where he'd first met Wallis Simpson.

"Can you imagine," Lily said later, after they'd returned to their suite, "giving up a kingdom for the woman you loved?"

"In a heartbeat," Connor agreed without hesitation.

Moved, she touched her lips to his and curled her arms around his neck, pressing her body against his. "Have I mentioned lately that I love you?"

"I seem to recall something about that." Connor's fingers settled at what was left of her waist. Her mouth was soft and warm as it toyed teasingly with his.

"Good. Because I do." She drew away again. Just slightly. "Love you." Her hands were busy at his throat; a moment later, Connor watched his tie flutter away. "Madly." His cream linen jacket followed.

He'd been planning to tell Lily the truth after dinner, before their return to the city tomorrow. But as she unbuttoned his shirt, pressing her lips against his chest, Connor felt all his good intentions slipping away.

"I love the way you taste." She tugged his shirt free and ran her hands across his back, causing needs to spread and grow inside him. "And feel." Returning to the task at hand, she began loosening his snowy cuffs.

Connor froze when she seemed briefly surprised by the gold cuff links, but the moment passed and his white shirt was soon lying on the brocade chair atop his jacket.

"Actually," Lily continued blithely, taking his hand and leading him to the bed, "I love everything about you."

Nudging him backward, onto the mattress, she took off his shoes. Once again Connor waited fatalistically for her to realize that ordinary handymen didn't tend to wear handmade Italian leather shoes, but, her mind set on seduction, she didn't notice.

She peeled his socks away. Then, unfastening his navy slacks, she drew them slowly down his legs, inch by inch, caressing the bared flesh with her hands, her lips.

When he was finally naked, totally exposed, Lily's warm gaze moved with infinite slowness over him. He'd never felt more vulnerable in his life than when her thoughtful eyes lingered for a long, heartfelt moment on his obvious arousal.

"Magnificent," she murmured silkily. She bent down and brushed her lips against the straining tip.

Then, backing up again, she unzipped the gauze dress she'd worn to the earthquake survival party. She stepped out of it, clad only in a silky teddy the color of freshly churned cream. He'd bought the sexy piece of lingerie in a chichi Rodeo Drive maternity shop catering to wealthy California girls who considered pregnancy a natural part of their sexuality.

Connor had liked the teddy when he'd first seen it hanging on its white satin cover. Now, viewing it on Lily, he liked it even better.

"Come here," he demanded. Hunger made his voice a husky growl.

With a sensual smile Lily did as instructed. She stood there, not moving as he reached out and cupped the warm silk at the juncture of her thighs. Moisture gathered as he stroked her with a knowing touch.

"I wanted to be the one to seduce you," Lily complained in a voice that was part honey, part smoke.

"You did." Desperate for a more intimate touch, he unfastened the snaps between her legs. "You are."

Her head was back, revealing a long slender throat. Her eyes were closed. Her hands were gripping his shoulders as if to keep from falling off the face of the earth.

"But seduction is a two-way street, Lily." When he slipped his finger into her moist warmth, her body, greedy for more, clutched desperately at his touch. Her hips began to move in concert with his stroking caress.

A red flush, like a fever, spread across her chest. Her eyes were glowing with a passion that matched his own. Her lips were parted, her breathing labored.

Watching as she neared climax, Connor decided she was the most glorious vision he'd ever seen.

"No!" She managed, with a ragged gasp, to free herself from his seductive touch. Determined to regain control, she straddled his dark thighs.

There was a flash of heat as she lowered her burning flesh onto him. Then, matching her fast, frantic rhythm, Connor allowed her to take them both into the flames.

"I DON'T THINK I'll ever move again." She was lying beside him, her smooth silky legs on either side of his, her lips at his throat.

"Sounds fine with me." He ran his hand down the damp flesh of her back. "But won't we eventually starve?"

She cuddled closer. He could feel her smile against his skin. "That's why God invented room service."

"Good point." As she lifted her head to smile up at him, Connor captured her mouth for a long, heartfelt kiss. "Lord, I love you." He couldn't keep the wonder from his tone. Or his worry.

"I know." The sweet innocence, laced with love shining in her eyes, made him once again feel about as low as a snake in a rut. "And that's what makes all this so special."

"That's part of it." He slipped his hand beneath the teddy they'd never bothered to take off and caressed her breast. "Being seduced wasn't bad, either."

She laughed, enjoying the moment. Enjoying Mac. When moisture from her nipple dampened the silk, she sighed.

"You realize, of course, that I have a doctor's appointment on Monday."

"Two o'clock." He'd already planned to leave the studio to take her to the Sunset Boulevard medical office.

"You realize, also, that she's probably going to tell me that we have to stop doing this."

"Doing what?" He bent his head and gathered in a shimmering drop of whitish fluid from the straining nipple. "This?" Yanking the silk over her head, he began treating her swollen breasts to a torment so sweet Lily thought she'd melt. "This?" His hand moved over her belly. With unerring accuracy, his clever fingers found the ultrasensitive kernel of flesh and began stroking it to renewed arousal. "Or this?"

How could she want him again so soon? After all they'd just shared? Lily tried to tell herself that her near constant desire for Mac these days was only rampaging hormones, but knew, deep down, that it was something else entirely. It was the man himself. And the love she felt for him.

"You know what I mean."

"I know." He kissed her. A long, drugging kiss that literally took her breath away. "But you're just talking about intercourse, Lily." His lips plucked enticingly at hers as he lay her back against the pillows. "There are lots of other ways to make love." His mouth roamed down her throat. Over her breasts. Her stomach. "Let me show you."

Which is exactly what he did. All night long.

"I hate to go back to the real world," Lily murmured as they drank a last cup of coffee in the luxurious Palm Court.

"I know the feeling." He still hadn't told her. Thinking back on his Mackay Silver King ancestry, Connor figured the old prospector would undoubtedly disown him for being such a coward.

"Look, it's not that long a drive back to L.A. How about we take a last walk along the beach? There's something important I have to say to you."

Although the weekend had been the most wonderful she'd ever known, Lily couldn't deny that deep down she was a little disappointed that she'd misjudged Mac's intention to propose. But now, as his fingers tightened painfully on hers, she realized that she hadn't been wrong, after all.

Loving him for being so nervous, when it should be obvious what her answer would be, Lily bestowed her warmest, most loving, most reassuring smile upon this man she intended to spend the rest of her life with.

"A walk sounds lovely."

They strolled across the lobby hand in hand. Once outside, they were heading down the steps, toward the sparkling silver sand when it happened.

"Connor?" a voice called out.

Connor froze. Lily, not recognizing the name, continued another step, pausing to look back at him. "Mac?"

"Connor, darling!" A voluptuous brunette had risen from one of the umbrella-topped tables on the terrace and was headed toward them like a steamship at full throttle. "What a surprise! What are you doing on Coronado?"

There was no point in trying to pretend to be a mere look-alike. Not when coming face-to-face with a woman he'd spent three passionate months with five years ago.

"Just taking a few days' vacation," he said, aware of Lily's confusion. Struggling to figure out how to extricate himself from the sticky, tangled web of deceit he'd woven around them, he introduced the women.

Kelly Donovan's brown eyes flicked over Lily with uncensored interest. "It's nice to meet you. Are you from the area?"

There was something going on here, Lily determined. Something she couldn't put her finger on. Although the woman seemed quite nice, Mac was literally radiating tension.

"I'm from Iowa, originally." Lily decided the gorgeous brunette must be one of Mac's old lovers. "These days I'm living in Los Angeles."

"Los Angeles?" A dark brow arched. "How nice." She turned to Connor. "Speaking of L.A.—"

He saw it coming. But from a long distance away, as if he were looking through the wrong end of a telescope. Time took on the slow-motion feel of an instant replay as Connor braced himself for the inevitable.

"Congratulations on this latest acquisition," Kelly was saying. "When I heard you were the new owner of Xanadu Studios, I remembered right away how much you loved going to movies and I said, that's our Connor. If they won't make the films he wants to see, he'll simply buy the place and make them himself."

He didn't, couldn't, immediately answer.

"I think you're mistaken," Lily said. "Mac works at Xanadu, but he certainly doesn't own the studio."

"Mac?" The intelligent brown eyes went from Lily's earnest face to Connor's stony one and back again. "Oh dear. I believe I hear my husband calling me," she murmured. "It was nice meeting you, Lily. Connor, good luck." With that she was gone.

As she watched Kelly Donovan escaping back to her table, Lily's whirling mind brought up a distressing sequence of past events.

She remembered Mac's initial statement that he'd come to Los Angeles on business, recalled the way he'd hedged about what he did for a living and how he'd been deliberately vague when she'd asked about his work at the studio.

She pictured last night's lovemaking, when she'd been undressing him, and had been momentarily surprised by his knotted gold cuff links. The twins of which she'd bought Junior at Tiffany's for their first anniversary.

"Mac?" She turned toward him. "What she said...about you and Xanadu ..." Her lovely face was as unnaturally pale as the day he'd pulled her from the surf. Her full lips were trembling.

"It's true." The words escaped on a long, ragged breath. "You're looking at the new owner of Xanadu Studios, Lily."

Even as she knew he was telling the truth, Lily was struggling against believing it. "But C. S. Mackay Enterprises bought the studio."

"I'm Connor Mackay. The *S* stands for Sullivan," he revealed on a low, flat tone.

"Oh, Lord." She pressed her trembling fingertips against her mouth.

Lily thought about all she'd learned about skip tracing. Had it only been Friday when she'd been so proud of her ability to uncover aliases? Obviously she was not nearly as clever as she thought. But then again, how could she have anticipated this man she'd been foolish enough to fall in love with was using a false identity?

"I trusted you." Her voice was thin. And fragile.

"I know." Feeling horribly clumsy, he reached out to stroke her hair. "But, in my defense, Lily, I had a reason for what I did. I know right now, it's coming as a shock, and—"

His attempted explanation was cut off by a sharp sound like a rifle retort. Lily stared at her hand, as if wondering how it had gotten on Mac—no, Connor's!—cheek.

"You lied to me." Her voice had gone as flat as her eyes, which reminded Connor of her candles being snuffed out by an icy wind.

She turned, preparing to leave, when Connor caught her by the arm. "Where are you going?"

"Back to L.A."

"You can't go there by yourself," he argued. "Not in your condition."

She pried his fingers from her sleeve. "We've been through this before. I'm not an invalid. I'm pregnant. Now, if you don't let me leave, right now, I'll start screaming. And your old lover can tell all your rich friends how your pregnant lover created a public scene."

There was enough ice coating her tone to cover Jupiter. Deciding that anger was better than the shock he'd first witnessed, Connor strangely welcomed whatever she wanted to do to him.

"I can understand why you might not want to drive back with me. But if you'll let me arrange for a car and driver—"

"No!" Her eyes were shooting angry sparks. "I won't take a cent from you, Mr. Mackay."

Her frigid formality, after a night of such hot intimacy, caused his own temper to flare. Reminding himself he deserved all this, and more, he tamped it down. "It'll be a loan."

"No."

"Look, you're entitled to be furious, Lily—"

"How generous of you to acknowledge that," she said between clenched teeth.

He ignored her sarcasm. "But if you won't think of yourself, at least think of your baby. You can't just go walking back to Los Angeles."

Although she hated to admit it, he had a point. "I'll take a cab to the bus station."

"How about the train? We can get you a compartment."

"*We* won't get me anything." She considered the idea. "But the train does sound more comfortable than a bus," she allowed. "I'll have the doorman call me a cab to take me to the station."

"I don't mind—"

"I do." She folded her arms across the bulge of her stomach. "I'm more than capable of taking care of myself and my baby, Mr. Mackay. So, if you don't mind, as nice a holiday as this has been, until your former girlfriend blew your cover, I'm going to have to ask you to butt out of my life."

She walked away without looking back.

Out of the hotel.

But not, Connor vowed, out of his life.

12

TWO DAYS AFTER Lily walked out of the Hotel Del Coronado, Connor was on Long Island, in the heart of Great Gatsby country, driving up a majestic, tree-lined drive that curved through acres of meadows, woods and rolling velvet lawns.

As twilight illuminated the sylvan landscape in a soft, amber glow, Connor could see the stone and slate exterior of Fairview, the Van Cortlandt family estate, rising in baronial splendor.

He parked beneath the wide porte cochere. The twelve foot high double doors were created of gleaming Honduras mahogany. When he pressed the button beside the door, from inside the house Connor could hear the peal of properly British Westminster chimes. The door was opened by a tall blond woman. Her nubby heather gray pleated slacks and white silk blouse portrayed the appearance of quiet wealth. As did the strand of very good pearls that echoed those adorning her earlobes. Her hair was cut in the same sleek society bob his mother had favored for as long as Connor could remember.

Indeed, by outward appearances, Madeline Van Cortlandt and Jessica Mackay could have been sisters. In reality, they could not have been more different. His mother, also born to wealth, was no snob. Indeed, she'd been thrilled to learn that Connor had found someone to love and even more excited about the idea of gaining a daughter-in-law and a grandchild in one fell swoop.

She'd never even thought to ask about Lily's family ties, and when Connor had volunteered the story about the Padgett family farm, her only comment was regret that it had fallen into bankruptcy and an idle curiosity as to whether Lily would want the family to buy it back. For vacations.

His mother was warm and loving and unhesitatingly generous. While Lily's former mother-in-law could make a rattlesnake seem warm-blooded by comparison.

"Connor!" She greeted him with a smile that somehow did not cause a single line around her lips or her eyes. "It was such a nice surprise when you called." She opened the door, inviting him into a two-story marble-floored foyer flanked by dual staircases. Her blue eyes swept over him. "You've grown."

"Since I was fourteen the last time you saw me, I'd say that was inevitable."

"Yes." She sighed. "You and Junior were roommates at the time. I remember thinking what a good influence you were on him.

Obviously not good enough, Connor considered as he followed her into a room of silk-draped walls, crystal sconces and crown molding.

"I was sorry to hear about his accident."

"It was a tragedy." The sun was setting. Outside the French doors, a pair of black swans glided tranquilly on a small, man-made lake. "But life goes on. Could I get you something to drink, Connor, dear? It is the cocktail hour."

Feeling as if he'd landed in a third-rate Noel Coward play, Connor said, "That really isn't necessary. Since I don't plan to be staying."

"I don't understand." She stopped in the act of pouring vodka from a Baccarat decanter into a cut crystal glass. "Why would you go to the trouble of driving all the way out here from the city, only to turn around and drive right back again?"

"I have a proposition to discuss with you."

"Oh, I'm afraid you've come at a bad time." Picking up a pair of silver tongs, she lifted an ice cube from a sterling bucket. "James Carter handles all the family business. And he's out of the country at the moment."

"I'm sure you're capable of passing on a message."

She glanced up at him, clearly surprised by the dangerous edge in his tone. "Of course."

"I want you to lay off Lily."

A blond brow climbed a forehead free of lines. "Excuse me?"

"You heard what I said. I want you to drop all this custody crap." With a silent apology to his mother for sinking to vulgarities, he crossed the room and looked down into her frigid face. "And most of all, I want you to leave Lily the hell alone."

Wealth had given the older woman a sense of privilege that served her well in times of stress. Without so much as blinking, she lifted her chin and said, "And what, may I ask, is Lily to you?"

"The woman I intend to marry."

That statement hit its mark. Madeline Van Cortlandt's mouth opened in a silent O of surprise.

"There's something you should probably know about me," Connor continued. "I'm incredibly protective about the people I love."

He had to give her credit for the speed with which she recovered. "Are you threatening me?"

"It's not a threat. It's a promise. If you don't call off your legal eagles right now, I'll keep you and your husband tied up in legal red tape until the kid is twenty-one and you've burned through every last penny of all the Van Cortlandt trust."

"There's not a judge in the land who couldn't see that Junior's child belongs here."

"*Lily's* child belongs with its mother. Your son never wanted his child."

"You can't know that!"

"I know what Lily's told me. I also think that running off with his mistress with their passports and half a million dollars in their luggage suggests he wasn't planning any father's day picnics any time soon."

She blanched beneath her Southampton tan. "How did you know about the money?"

"Lily told me."

"And you believe her? A common farm girl with absolutely no background?"

"I believe Lily without question," Connor responded. "But it just so happens that a friend of mine on Wall Street confirmed the unpleasant fact that Junior had gone beyond churning his clients' accounts to embezzling funds from their portfolios."

"That's a lie!"

It was the truth. And they both knew it.

"It's your choice, Madeline." Connor was growing bored with the company and the conversation. "Leave Lily alone and you can create whatever rosy myth you want about your deceased son. One more threatening letter, any more intimidating phone calls or even a Christmas card and I will make your life a living hell."

"You have no right talking to me that way." The formerly icy blue eyes flashed. The thin lips trembled with barely restrained temper. "Your parents obviously did not teach you proper behavior toward your elders, Connor."

"That may be, Mrs. Van Cortlandt," he agreed easily. "But they taught me something even more important. Although our roots in this country may not go back to the founding fathers, believe me, lady, if there's one thing we Mackays do well, it's protect our own. Lily's one of us now. And don't forget it."

Satisfied that he'd made his point, he said, "Don't bother to see me out. I can find my way."

As he left the mansion, Connor was whistling.

A WEEK AFTER the breakup, Lily's two best friends surprised her with a baby shower. The outpouring of affection and support from the women of Bachelor Arms—not to mention the loot for the baby—made her cry.

After everyone left, she was sitting with Blythe and Cait in her apartment, surrounded by discarded pink and blue wrapping paper. Lily had been planning, all evening, to break the news that she was entering into a partnership with Gage, but the opportunity hadn't arisen during the festive party.

Now, before she could say a word, Cait, with her usual knack for not beating around the bush, set the agenda for the evening's discussion.

"Don't you think you're being awfully hard on him?"

"Hard on who?" Lily asked with feigned confusion. "Mac? Or Connor the lying-snake-in-the-grass Mackay?"

"Come on, Lily," Cait coaxed. "Surely during that year of law school you learned that even rich venture capitalists are innocent until proven guilty."

Despite the festive party, and the reason to celebrate her renewed good fortune, Lily was feeling cranky from lack of sleep. If the baby's increased acrobatics didn't keep her awake at night, leg cramps and back aches did. Although she'd never admit it, as her due date grew closer, she found herself missing Mac's—no, Connor's, she reminded herself firmly—soothing massages.

She was also not thrilled by the way Blythe and Cait continued to try to defend Connor's behavior.

"He lied," she insisted.

"Yes, he did," Blythe agreed calmly. "But his motives weren't entirely self-serving, Lily."

"That's right," Cait said with a vigorous nod that sent her fiery waves dancing. "In the beginning, he just didn't want to upset you by bringing up that failed business deal with Junior. Then it just all got out of hand. He's really miserable without you, Lily."

"It sounds as if you two have been talking with him lately."

Lily was not surprised. Disappointed. But not surprised. She also refused to ask where he was living. After she'd refused to open her door to him, he'd left Bachelor Arms. And except for the presents that continued to come every day—gifts she continued to refuse—she hadn't heard a word from him.

"I can't help running into him at the studio," Blythe said, sounding somewhat defensive.

"And Sloan and I had dinner with him last night," Cait allowed.

"You had dinner with him? You and Sloan?" That was a surprise. "I thought you were my friend!"

"I am." Cait pulled out her no-nonsense cop stare. "But this isn't sixth grade, Lily. Just because you refuse to talk to the guy doesn't mean I'm being unforgivably disloyal if I do. Besides," she said, "I happen to like Connor. A lot."

Lily's response was forestalled by a knock on the door. One she'd come to expect. "Here we go again," she muttered. She opened the door, barely glancing at the package the delivery man was holding. "You can take this one back, too."

"Oh, no, you don't!" Cait said, jumping up as she recognized the gold box of Belgian chocolates. Flashing the delivery man a bright, dazzling smile, she signed for the candy.

"Now he's going to think I'm caving in," Lily complained.

"I'll confess everything tomorrow." Opening the box, Cait bit into a strawberry truffle, rolled her eyes and said, "The man has delicious taste." She passed the box to Blythe, who pulled out a piece of white chocolate shaped like a starfish. And to Lily who, unable to resist, reluctantly succumbed to the appeal of a piece of creamy milk chocolate.

"If I wasn't already madly in love with Sloan, I'd marry Connor Mackay just for these," Cait said, licking chocolate off her fingers. "And expensive candy aside, Lily, I'm sticking to my first impression that he's just the man for you."

"I've already been married to one rich man," Lily reminded her. "And look how that turned out."

Cait swore. Lily decided she must have picked up the extremely earthy, pungent curse during her days patrolling the streets.

"Exactly how much money would Connor have to give away?" Blythe asked with her usual commonsense approach to things. "Before you'd be willing to give him a second chance?"

"It's a moot point," Lily muttered, refusing to fall into the trap. "Since we both know he never would."

"Perhaps not." Blythe's dark eyes moved with overt concern over Lily's face. From her slight frown, Lily suspected that the extra cover-up beneath her eyes wasn't exactly camouflaging the deep shadows as well as she'd hoped. "But he's the same man he was when you fell in love with him, Lily. The same man who fell in love with you."

"He didn't love me. He was just playing a game, using me as some kind of sick distraction." Even as she heard the words leave her mouth, Lily knew they weren't true.

"You paint a very unpleasant picture of wealth," Blythe commented mildly. "Is that how you see me? As someone who's been pretending to like you for my own amusement these past eight years?"

"Of course not!" Lily was stunned Blythe could even consider a thing. "You're not like other rich people. You're different."

"I'm not like the Van Cortlandts," Blythe agreed.

"And neither is Connor," Cait insisted. "And if you weren't so busy trying to paint both men with the same brush, you'd see that for yourself."

The truth of that accusation hit a little too close to home. "I don't want to talk about Connor Mackay," Lily insisted. "Not tonight. Because I have something else to tell you."

The argument was put aside when she broke her news. Her two best friends were as happy for her as she'd hoped.

The conversation remained bright and positive. Toasts were made, jokes told, gossip shared. It was, to all outward appearances, a successful evening.

But later, after Blythe and Cait had left, Lily went into the room she'd been preparing for her baby, sat down in the used rocking chair she still hadn't gotten around to refinishing, and wept.

"YOU'RE GOING TO LOVE this one," the woman Connor had been spending several hours each day with promised. As they left the Pacific Coast Highway at Malibu's Point Dume, she flashed him a smile as bright as the sunshine on the water.

"I hope so," he muttered. A man accustomed to making quick decisions, Connor was growing weary of being dragged all over Los Angeles in search of the perfect house.

Not wanting to upset Lily so close to delivery, and deciding that it might be a good idea to give her time to cool down, Connor had moved into the suite at the Century Plaza, as he'd originally planned.

The waiting wasn't easy. If it hadn't been for the continued encouragement from Blythe and Cait that Lily would eventually see the light, he would have been camped out on her doorstep.

Today's offering was perched atop a spectacular wide sandy beach bluff. The moment he saw it, Connor knew he was home.

"Despite the size, it's really quite comfortable," the realtor assured him as she cut the Mercedes's engine. "And there are views from every room." Even from the driveway, the bright peacock blue waters of the ocean provided a spectacular vista.

Inside, the house was open and inviting, elegant and serene. The realtor's high heels tapped briskly on the peach-hued terra cotta floor as she displayed the highlights of the spacious home.

"This is the game room," she said, opening a pair of double doors onto a room that boasted a green-felted pool table, wet bar, an audio and video entertainment center that took up one wall, a towering stone fireplace and, wonderfully, Connor thought, an enormous train set.

"Does that come with the place?" he asked, studying the amazingly detailed replica of a Swiss village atop the table.

"The owner's offering the home furnished." The realtor reiterated what she'd already told him in the car on the drive up here. "Everything's negotiable."

Connor pictured a small, miniature version of Lily, sitting on a stool beside him, wearing a striped engineer's hat atop her blond head as she operated the controls. The image was more than a little appealing. "The train stays."

"Fine." She nodded, obviously realizing that she was about to close what could well be her biggest sale of the month. "It really is quite charming." She opened a teak case, revealing a command center that looked as if it belonged at Cape Canaveral. "Would you like to try it out?"

Feeling seven years old again, Connor spent the next five minutes sending the train roaring through alpine tunnels, over bridges, up snowy mountainsides. After reluctantly bringing the engine back to the station, he decided he would have bought the house for this setup alone.

Continuing the tour, the realtor led him into an adjoining room that was obviously an exercise room. The mirrored walls reflected back a vast array of equipment. The sauna's in there," she said with a wave of her hand toward a thick door. "It's wonderfully cozy."

He glanced in at the wood-walled room and imagined making love to Lily on one of the wooden benches. "I like it."

The rooms flowed gracefully, from one giant ocean-front sweep to another. Connor walked through the expansive kitchen with its state-of-the-art appliances and granite counters into the adjoining dining room, where he thought about making love to Lily on the table designed to seat eighteen.

"This is the master suite." The woman opened a door onto a vast, yet charming combination bedroom, bath and sitting room. Wicker and chintz predominated; Connor knew Lily would love it.

"As you can see, the French doors open onto the swimming pool," the realtor pointed out. "Which in turn overlooks the ocean."

The only problem Connor could foresee with the suite would be deciding where to make love to Lily first—in the romantic four-poster bed draped with gossamer white netting or in the blue-and-white tiled pool.

"I'll take it," Connor said. "On one condition."

"Which is?"

"I need the large guest room redone."

"That certainly shouldn't be a problem, I'm sure we can find a decorator who would be able to do the job sometime this summer."

"That's not good enough. I need it converted into a dream nursery within the next three days."

Her poppy red lips turned down in a frown. "I don't know if—"

"I'm willing to pay," Connor said, with a slight mental apology to Lily. "Whatever it takes." There were times, and this was one of them, that having some bucks to throw around proved a decided advantage.

Her smile was bright and professional. "I'm sure we can work out something."

THE FIRST PAIN came before dawn. Believing it to be yet another occurrence of the false labor that had sent her rushing off to the doctor the day before, Lily ignored it.

The twinges continued from time to time during the day, but she was kept too busy to pay them much heed. The phones didn't stop ringing.

"Harold says that the pod people have landed in Hollywood and taken over the cast of 'The Guiding Light,'" she informed Gage when he returned from a stakeout.

Although he didn't like doing matrimonial work, the job was for a former client. At this point in his career, Gage couldn't afford to be choosy. "The full moon always brings out the wackos," he muttered. Two hours sitting in a car, watching the door of a motel room wasn't exactly his idea of an ideal way to spend an sunny afternoon.

"When I told Harold I thought 'The Guiding Light' was taped on the east coast, he decided he really meant 'The Young and The Restless.'" Lily grinned. "I promised to call the director and warn him that he was dealing with aliens.

"Oh, and Blythe wants to talk to you. She asked if you could call her whenever you came in."

He frowned, knowing he was in trouble when just hearing her name could cause a frisson of expectation. "Did she say what she wanted?"

"No." Another pain, stronger than any she'd experienced thus far wrenched her back and sent her abdomen into spasms.

Her ragged gasp captured Gage's immediate attention. "How long has this been going on?"

She breathed easier as the pain abated. "Since morning. They started about four, but I didn't think they were real."

Gage remembered his rookie year when he'd delivered a baby in the back of his patrol car on the San Diego freeway at rush hour. "That sure as hell looked real enough to me. Let's go."

"To the hospital?" Although she never would have thought it possible, after having waited for nine long months for this day, Lily was suddenly not eager to progress to the next stage.

"Unless you intend to have your baby on the floor between phone calls from lunar crackpots."

Of all the reasons Lily had come to like Gage, his absolute unflappability was one of the highest on her list. That and the fact that he was a genuinely caring man.

Another pain hit. Hard. "I suppose it's too late to change my mind." Vowing to remain calm, she waited for the contraction to subside, then took his outstretched hand and struggled out of the chair. "We might as well get this show on the road."

Connor was about to give a scheduled press conference concerning his plans for the future of Xanadu when Blythe called with the news that Lily was in labor. Leaving the assembled reporters, he ran out of the studio.

He was driving like a maniac, breaking every speeding law on the books, when a CHP motorcycle cop pulled him over just before he'd reached the Sunset off-ramp. Fortunately, the giant wearing the uniform of authority and storm trooper boots turned out to be a father of six, who upon learning that it was Connor's first baby, assured him that he had plenty of time, reminded him that it wouldn't do his wife any good for him to end up in an accident, then sent him on his way with a warning.

The birthing room had been designed to calm fears and ease anxiety. Yellow rosebuds climbed up white trellises on the wallpapered walls, lace curtains covered the windows, letting in a buttery sunshine while blocking off the less than inspiring view of the asphalt parking lot.

Propped up in bed against a pile of pillows, Lily was surrounded by friends when Connor came strolling in the door as if nothing had happened between them.

"Someone call for a coach?" he asked in a mild tone that belied the wild, out-of-control pounding of his heart.

Never having been one to hold grudges for very long, Lily wasn't about to start now. Not when she was so honestly relieved to see Mac. Connor, she reminded herself.

"You're late."

Relief flooded over him in cooling waves. Connor could feel the tension literally draining from his body. "I got held up."

He walked toward her, his gaze riveted on her face. She'd obviously been working hard; her blond hair was drenched in perspiration and she'd chewed angry marks into her bottom lip.

She couldn't take her eyes from this man she'd thought she'd lost. This man she'd stubbornly, foolishly sent away. This man she loved.

"Better late than never," she said.

The uncensored love he saw shining in her sapphire eyes made his hopes soar. Just as he reached her side, another contraction swept over her and she began to pant in quick, short, energy-draining gasps.

He sat down on the edge of the bed and looked straight into her eyes. "Deep breath, remember?"

His voice was deep and warm and soothing. As were his hands as they began massaging her abdomen, which hardened with the contraction.

"Slow and deep." He began to breathe with her, encouraging her to relax. "Nice and easy." His hands stroked outward and upward toward her hip bones. "We've plenty of time, sweetheart." As she became strangely hypnotized by the commanding gleam in his eyes, Lily's breathing gradually slowed.

As Lily and Connor shared the intensely intimate moment, the others, wanting to give the couple some much needed privacy, slipped unnoticed from the room.

Connor had been to the classes. Watched the films. He'd even reread the book three times in the past two days, preparing for this event. But nothing had prepared him for the sight of the woman he loved in such obvious pain.

Reminding himself that his job was to ease her discomfort, not add to it with his own, he forced himself to remain calm.

"That's it," he crooned encouragingly. "You're doing great." His fingertips were like magic wands, soothing the pressure, easing her pain. "This is going to be a walk in the park," he promised.

"You're as big a liar as the nurse who taught the damn class," Lily accused through clenched teeth. The contraction passed. She lay back against the pillows.

Her face was glistening with fresh sweat. Her hair was hanging limp around her shoulders. She was, without a doubt, the most beautiful woman Connor had ever seen.

"I'm sorry." This was not the time for excuses or explanations, but he felt it needed to be said.

"I know."

Although she'd already decided to forgive him as little as two hours ago, Lily had been looking forward to making him crawl. Just a little. But now, on the verge of bringing a new life into the world, she realized what he'd done, and his reasons for having done it, no longer mattered.

What was important was that she loved him. That he loved her. And that they'd both love this child.

"I brought you a present." Reaching into his pocket, he pulled out a gray velvet box. As he held it out to her, he felt as nervous as a teenager asking a girl out on a first date.

Suddenly as nervous as he, Lily opened the box with trembling fingers.

"Oh, Mac," she breathed on a soft sigh, as she viewed the gold band that featured two hands clasping a heart. "It's lovely."

"It was my great-grandmother's." It was going to be all right, Connor realized. *They* were going to be all right. "My great-grandfather brought it over on the boat with him from County Tipperary for his bride."

Watching her face carefully, he said, "I knew you'd already had diamonds." Cait had also told him how she'd sold them to pay off her husband's debts. "I wanted to give you something from the heart."

Her eyes misted. Knowing that he could probably afford the Hope diamond and realizing that he understood that family meant more to her than money ever could, made this heirloom even more special.

His next words reminded her how often she'd thought Mac could read her mind. "By the way, my mother can't wait to meet you. She's also on cloud nine about becoming a grandmother. In fact, when I talked to her last night, she'd just gotten home from a class on cooking natural baby food."

He slipped the ring on her finger. Then bent down and gave her a long, deep, drugging kiss that was sweeter than any they'd shared.

"You are going to let me make an honest woman of you, aren't you?"

Lily laughed, even as she felt another contraction beginning to swell. "Far be it from me to disappoint your mother."

The afternoon ripened, dusk fell, night draped its velvet cloak over the city as Lily worked to bring her baby into the world.

Connor never left her side, proving a wellspring of support as he massaged her abdomen and back, stroked her arms and legs, wiped her face with cool cloths, moistened her throat and lips with chips of ice, helped her stay calm, and, most importantly, cheered her on.

For the early part of the evening, the others would take turns visiting. Then finally, it was time.

"You're doing great, sweetheart," Connor said, breathing in rhythm with her quick pants. "Just a little bit more."

"Let's have another push, Lily," the doctor said. "The baby's about to crown."

Her head swimming from the effort, Lily bore down.

"Look, Lily." Connor lifted their joined hands and pointed toward the mirror that allowed them to watch the birth. "You can see the baby's head."

Stirred by the sight, Lily took a deep breath and on a deep-throated moan, pushed harder, bracing herself for another wave of pain.

"It's out." The doctor's tone was briskly pleased. "Okay, Lily, the hard work is over now. From here on in, it's going to be a cakewalk."

Lily was drenched in sweat. The scrub shirt Connor had donned for the birth was drenched as well. More sweat dripped off his forehead onto their linked hands. Neither Connor nor Lily noticed. All their attention was directed toward the amazing sight of those little eyes, nose, mouth and chin.

"It's got hair," Connor said on a note of wonder.

"Of course my child has hair," Lily said indignantly, unwilling to admit that she was as amazed as he by the wet black fuzz.

"I thought babies were supposed to be bald. Like Winston Churchill."

"Don't make me laugh," Lily complained, caught between laughter and tears. "Not now." She began to pant again. "And for the record, my baby is beautiful."

"That's what my mother always said about me." Connor brushed some damp hair off her forehead. "My father, on the other hand, said I looked a great deal like Uncle Fester."

Another laugh eased the pain. Seconds later the pressure abated as the baby slid from her womb with a silky ease. "What is it?" Lily and Connor asked together.

"You're the proud parents of a lovely baby girl," the doctor announced.

"Oh, my God!" Tears welled up in Lily's eyes, then brimmed over. "A little girl."

"We have a daughter." The thought was as stunning as it was thrilling. His eyes as wet as Lily's, Connor brushed the tears from her cheeks with his thumb. "Thank you."

As the loud, indignant wail of new life echoed around them, Connor bent his head and pressed his lips against Lily's.

The wiggling infant was placed at Lily's breast and immediately began suckling on a nipple. She really was a mother, Lily thought. Life was incredible.

"A miracle," Connor murmured. He'd never witnessed a more powerfully emotional sight.

Bringing her daughter into the world had taken hours. She should be exhausted. But instead, Lily couldn't remember ever having been more exhilarated.

"Yes." As she stroked the top of her child's head, Lily watched the flash of gold and thought about all the generations of love those clasped hands represented.

Two months ago, she'd been alone in the world, without any family to celebrate her triumphs and support her when she was down. But now, amazingly, she had a daughter. And soon, a husband who loved her. She even had a mother-in-law eager to cook baby food.

It didn't matter that Mac was wealthy. She'd feel exactly the same way if he'd turned out to be the out-of-work carpenter she'd thought she'd fallen in love with. Because so long as they had each other—and their child—they'd be the richest people on earth.

Lily smiled up at him, her love-filled heart shining in her eyes. "It seems to be a night for miracles."

A miracle.

Alexandra's head was spinning as she left the doctor's office on Sunset Boulevard. It couldn't be true. But it was. The rabbit had died. She was pregnant. Eight weeks to be exact.

Having been told she could not conceive, Alexandra had resigned herself to never having children. When she'd shared her secret shame with Patrick, he'd quickly, in his direct western way, assured her that it didn't matter. That he had plenty of brood mares back on his ranch in Wyoming. He didn't need to marry one.

And now his child was growing inside her. Despite the problems this would cause at Xanadu, despite the fact that

*Walter Stern would be livid, joy bubbled through her,
sparkling in her veins like champagne.*

*Laughing, Alexandra pressed her hand against her still
flat stomach and imagined she could feel their baby stir.*

*Then she went home to tell her husband that he was
about to become a father.*

* * * * *

Coming up in Bachelor Arms—
*When Blythe Fielding planned her wedding and
asked her two best friends, Caitlin and Lily, to be
bridesmaids, none of them had a clue a new
romance was around the corner for each of them—
even the bride! These entertaining, dramatic
stories of friendship, mystery and love by JoAnn
Ross continue the exploits of the residents of
Bachelor Arms and answer one very important
question: Will Blythe ever walk down the aisle?*
Find out in
THREE GROOMS AND A WEDDING
(July 1995, #545)

*Soon to move into Bachelor Arms
are the heroes and heroines in books by popular
authors Candace Schuler and Judith Arnold.
Don't miss their stories!*

HARLEQUIN®
Temptation®

Secret Fantasies

Do you have a secret fantasy?

America's sweetheart Josie Eastman does. She's always done what she's told, never endangered her precious career. And she's sick of it. So she drops everything and escapes into the arms of a bad-boy rancher. But soon she realizes why she was always told, "Never love a cowboy...." Enjoy #546 NEVER LOVE A COWBOY by Kate Hoffmann, available in July 1995.

Everybody has a secret fantasy. And you'll find them all in Temptation's exciting new yearlong miniseries, Secret Fantasies. Beginning January 1995, one book each month focuses on the hero and heroine's innermost romantic desires....

SF-7

Take 4 bestselling love stories FREE

Plus get a FREE surprise gift!

Special Limited-time Offer

Mail to Harlequin Reader Service®

> 3010 Walden Avenue
> P.O. Box 1867
> Buffalo, N.Y. 14269-1867

YES! Please send me 4 free Harlequin Temptation® novels and my free surprise gift. Then send me 4 brand-new novels every month, which I will receive before they appear in bookstores. Bill me at the low price of $2.44 each plus 25¢ delivery and applicable sales tax, if any.* That's the complete price and a savings of over 10% off the cover prices—quite a bargain! I understand that accepting the books and gift places me under no obligation ever to buy any books. I can always return a shipment and cancel at any time. Even if I never buy another book from Harlequin, the 4 free books and the surprise gift are mine to keep forever.

142 BPA AJHR

Name	(PLEASE PRINT)	
Address	Apt. No.	
City	State	Zip

This offer is limited to one order per household and not valid to present Harlequin Temptation® subscribers. *Terms and prices are subject to change without notice. Sales tax applicable in N.Y.

UTEMP-295   ©1990 Harlequin Enterprises Limited

HARLEQUIN®

Temptation

BACHELOR ARMS SURVEY

SET THE SCENE!

Pick your spot for the world's best marriage proposal

1. You and your love at home curled up in front of a roaring fire.
2. You and he alone on top of a mountain you've just hiked with the world spread out below you.
3. He whisks you away to a tropical island for a long weekend and proposes on the beach at sunset.
4. He pulls out a gorgeous ring at a wonderful restaurant and, after you accept, the waiters burst into song and pour champagne to the deafening applause.
5. At a surprise party for you on Valentine's Day with all your friends and family in attendance.

We want to hear from you, so please send in your response to:

> In the U.S.: BACHELOR ARMS,
> P.O. Box 9076, Buffalo, NY 14269-9076

> In Canada: BACHELOR ARMS,
> P.O. Box 637, Ft. Erie, ON L2A 5X3

Name: _____

Address:_____ City:_____

State/Prov.:_____ Zip/Postal Code:_____

Please note that all entries become the property of Harlequin and we may publish them in any publication with credit at our discretion.

THREE BESTSELLING AUTHORS

HEATHER GRAHAM POZZESSERE
THERESA MICHAELS
MERLINE LOVELACE

bring you

THREE HEROES THAT DREAMS ARE MADE OF!

The Highwayman——He knew the honorable thing was to send his captive home, but how could he let the beautiful Lady Kate return to the arms of another man?

The Warrior——Raised to protect his tribe, the fierce Apache warrior had little room in his heart until the gentle Angie showed him the power and strength of love.

The Knight——His years as a mercenary had taught him many skills, but would winning the hand of a spirited young widow prove to be his greatest challenge?

Don't miss these **UNFORGETTABLE RENEGADES!**

Available in August wherever Harlequin books are sold.

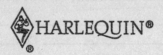

HARLEQUIN®

HREN

In June, get ready for thrilling romances and FREE BOOKS—Western-style— with...

WESTERN *Lovers*

You can receive the first 2 Western Lovers titles FREE!

June 1995 brings Harlequin and Silhouette's WESTERN LOVERS series, which combines larger-than-life love stories set in the American West! And WESTERN LOVERS brings you stories with your favorite themes... "Ranch Rogues," "Hitched In Haste," "Ranchin' Dads," "Reunited Hearts" the packaging on each book highlights the popular theme found in each WESTERN LOVERS story!

And in June, when you buy either of the Men Made In America titles, you will receive a WESTERN LOVERS title absolutely FREE! Look for these fabulous combinations:

♦ Buy ALL IN THE FAMILY
   by Heather Graham Pozzessere (Men Made In America) and receive a FREE copy of
   BETRAYED BY LOVE by Diana Palmer
   (Western Lovers)

♦ Buy THE WAITING GAME
   by Jayne Ann Krentz (Men Made In America) and receive a FREE copy of
   IN A CLASS BY HIMSELF by JoAnn Ross
   (Western Lovers)

Look for the special, extra-value shrink-wrapped packages at your favorite retail outlet!

HARLEQUIN® ® Silhouette® TM

WL-T

Announcing
the New Pages & Privileges™ Program
from Harlequin® and Silhouette®

Get All This FREE
With Just One Proof-of-Purchase!

- **FREE Hotel Discounts** of up to 60% off at leading hotels in the U.S., Canada and Europe

- **FREE Travel Service** with the guaranteed lowest available airfares plus 5% cash back on every ticket

- **FREE $25 Travel Voucher** to use on any ticket on any airline booked through our Travel Service

- **FREE Petite Parfumerie** collection (a $50 Retail value)

- **FREE Insider Tips Letter** full of fascinating information and hot sneak previews of upcoming books

- **FREE Mystery Gift** (if you enroll before June 15/95)

And there are more great gifts and benefits to come!
Enroll today and become Privileged!

(see insert for details)

 # PROOF-OF-PURCHASE

Offer expires October 31, 1996   HT-PP2